The Romance of the Secret Service Fund by Fred M White

Fred Merrick White was born in 1859 in West Bromwich in the Midlands of England to Joseph White and Helen Merrick who had married the previous year.

Joseph was a solicitor's managing clerk, who by the time the family moved to Hereford a few years later, had become a solicitor's article clerk.

Little is known of White's early years but what is known is that he followed in his father's footsteps and worked as a solicitor's clerk in Hereford. His father by now had also become a solicitor and times seemed quite prosperous for the family.

However in the late 1880's something went badly wrong for his father and he was imprisoned.

White had by now decided that writing was a more preferable career for him than the law. By 1891 Fred M. White, now 31 years old, was working full-time as a journalist and author, earning enough to support himself and his mother, Helen. By this time Fred's younger brother, Joseph A. White, had left home and working as a glass-blower.

In 1892, White married Clara Jane Smith. The wedding took place at King's Norton, Worcestershire, and the couple went on to have two children; Sydney Eric White (1893) and Ormond John White (1895).

As the century closed Fred's father had been released from prison and was living as a "retired solicitor", together with Helen, in Worthington in West Sussex.

By the time of the 1911 census, Fred M. White, now 52 years old, and his wife Clara were living at Uckfield, a town in the Wealden district of East Sussex. As the ominous shadows of the First World War gathered White had established himself as a popular and extremely prolific author. Indeed whether it was novels or short stories they flowed from his pen with a startling speed and many of them were initially serialized in the popular weekly and monthly magazines. His clever use of science to create imaginative and highly adventurous story lines was a particular talent of his.

During the First World War, both of his sons served as junior officers in The Royal Inniskilling Fusiliers.

The titanic struggle of the First World War and his sons' war-time experiences in it greatly influenced this phase of his writing. His novel The Seed of Empire (1916), describes early trench warfare in great and gritty detail. He went on to describe how the social changes after the war created many problems for returning soldiers as they attempted to fit back into a now peaceful society.

Fred and Clara spent their twilight years in Barnstaple in Devon, an area which also provided the backdrop for his novels The Mystery Of Crocksands, The Riddle Of The Rail, and The Shadow Of The Dead Hand.

Fred Merrick White died in Barnstaple in 1935.

Index of Contents

BY WOMAN'S WIT

"Go to death; go to death; go to death; go to death. Your wife's a bride; your wife's a bride. Go to death; go to death; go to death; go to death. Your wife's a bride; your wife's a bride."

The mad refrain was hammered into Newton Moore's brain by the clang and roar of the flashing miles. A vivid streak of gold and crimson, enveloped in a cloud of vapor, crashed on over the silver-white metals—the fiery trail that men called the South East European Express.

The voice of the big compound engine spoke thus to Newton Moore. To all practical purposes he was going to his death, and was not his wife a bride still? The most valued and trusted servant of the British Secret Service Fund had kissed his wife once upon the lips, and turned his white face to the East at the bidding of his chief.

"It's the toughest job you ever had," Sir Gresham Welby had told him. "But come what may, you must get to the bottom of this business, or share the fate of Rigby and Long and Mercer. You have a free hand, and the whole of the resources of the Secret Service Fund behind you."

Moore had shuddered. He was a man cursed with a vivid imagination, and unseen terrors always unmanned him. But it was when Moore was face to face with danger that he rose so triumphantly over circumstances. He had described himself as a coward, who was a hero in spite of himself. His imagination magnified the unseen danger, but the same fine inventiveness taught him the right moment to strike.

"Are you really equal to the task?" Sir Gresham had asked suddenly.

It seemed to him that Moore looked slight and pale. His pince-nez gave him a certain suggestion of mildness.

"I don't know any other man on the staff who can undertake it," he said. "And this is no ordinary matter. Three of the best men we have ever had have been murdered mysteriously, and we are no nearer the solution of the problem than before. And yet there is not so very much to find out."

"I agree with you, Moore. We are almost ready to vouch for the integrity of Prince Boris of Contigua, and yet we know that Russia is using the Court and province to foment disaffection on the Indian frontier, and convey arms to the Mancunis. If this thing isn't stopped we shall be face to face with the most serious trouble in India before long. Signs are not wanting, too, that the Contigeans are being stirred up against Prince Boris. If there is a revolution, Russia has a fine excuse to step in and annex the province. And you know as well as I do what that would mean."

"I do," Moore replied, "and I know the country well. My last novel was founded upon Contigean politics. Princess Natalie was very pleased with the book. And I am quite sure that she is on our side."

"You are a curious mixture of a man," said Sir Gresham. "Let us hope that your imagination will find some solution of the problem. We want no more tragedies. And remember that you have an absolutely free hand. Let us know who is working the mischief and we ask no more. For the present you are practically the embodiment of the Secret Service Fund."

And now Moore was reaching his destination. Three of the bravest men he had ever served with had perished on the same mission, dying in a manner so mysterious that Her Majesty's Government were powerless to fix the blame on anyone. They had been struck down one after the other, barely before they had set foot in Tenedos, the capital of Contigua, and, for aught he knew to the contrary, the same fate awaited him twenty miles away.

For the present he was horribly frightened. Passive danger always rendered him almost physically sick. His imagination thrilled him. He could not eat, he could do no more than smoke his ubiquitous cigarettes.

Presently the long rocking line of red and gold came vibrating to a standstill, for the frontier was reached and the weary business of the Customs had to be undertaken. All this was as nothing to Moore, for his baggage had been marked through two days before. He tumbled out of the carriage and made his way to the grimy refreshment-room, where little beyond coffee and crackers could be obtained.

"I must worry something down," he muttered. "I've had nothing for thirty hours. I wonder if I could manage a cracker."

One waiter only was in attendance. He brought hot coffee of acrid flavor and two large flat crackers on a platter. One of the thin flour cakes Moore managed, but he dubiously eyed the other. Listlessly he crumbled it with his finger. Some foreign substance—paper—fell out upon the plate. Moore grew rigid with a sudden comprehension. A less imaginative man would have ordered another cracker. Moore scented a plot here. He smoothed out the scrap of paper, and surely enough there was a message there.

"Do not take this train on to Tenedos," it ran. "Contrive to miss it. In the village you can manage to obtain post horses to your destination. Do not start before six o'clock in the evening, and you will reach Tenedos by midnight. Ask to be directed to the large inn on the Varna Road."

There was not much time to decide. The letter might come from the hand of a friend or equally from the hand of an enemy. Moore decided to act upon the impulse that seldom played him false. He remained.

The polyglot language of the country was no sealed book to him. Within an hour he was safely housed at the large rambling building on the Varna Road, where he had found it possible to obtain a pair of horses to take him to Tenedos later on in the day.

It might have been mere suspicion on the part of Moore, but it seemed to him that the obese old landlord with the silver rings in his ears was not altogether surprised at the advent of his visitor. The former's fat countenance lacked repose, his little eyes followed Moore restlessly.

"His Excellency would like a private room?" he more than suggested.

Moore nodded carelessly. He was quite prepared to play the game according to the rules. A big, low apartment with dark panels was insufficiently lighted by two dreary candles in brass sconces. The atmosphere was dark and heavy. Moore turned the key in the lock, and hardly had he done so when another door opened and a woman entered.

The Princess stood before him, dark, beautiful, palpitating with emotion—a lovely woman with a history, an ambitious woman with a scorching hatred of Russia, and burning with a love for her own sterile country.

"Listen to me," she said. "I knew that you were coming, but, what is more to the point, others know it also. Had you gone on to Tenedos as arranged, you would have been a dead man before morning. How glad, glad I am that you accepted my warning."

"It was a sufficiently vague one, your Highness," said Moore.

"Because I could not make it more definite. If you only knew the system of espionage by which I am hampered! There is a traitor in the camp, and that traitor has obtained a prevailing influence at the Court. The Prince is utterly in his power, and he is making the most unscrupulous use of his advantage. And, worse than all, he is an agent of Russia."

All this Moore was quite prepared to hear. As Agent of the Secret Service Fund, it was his duty to come here and expose the Russian spy who was working all the mischief. This done, his task was practically complete. But, at the same time, he fully appreciated the danger that lay before him.

"Your Highness is running a risk in coming here," he suggested.

"To a certain extent, yes. But when I accidentally discovered that you were the Agent chosen by the British Government, I knew that it must be now or never. I arranged a hunting party for to-day close here, and so I managed to elude the rest of my party. The people here are faithful and devoted to my service. In a few moments I must slip away again and join the others.

"By missing your train you have for the time being baffled those who would destroy you. Under ordinary circumstances, they will not expect you now till to-morrow evening. You will lie quiet on your arrival, and late to-morrow afternoon advise the Prince that you are in Tenedos. Then you will be asked to join us at dinner to-morrow night. After that everything depends upon your nerve and courage. If you are brave you will not only gain your point, but you will absolutely save Contigua as well. It will be in your hands to expose Zouroff and render him powerless for the future. And as to his wife, she shall be my care."

Even in the dim light Princess Natalie's eyes flashed. This woman was moved by a chord more dominant even than her patriotism—by tbe desire to be avenged upon a woman who had wronged her.

"So Zouroff is the god in the car," Moore observed. "A marvellously clever man, and absolutely unscrupulous. They say his wife is beyond compare."

"She is certainly amazingly lovely," the Princess admitted, "so lovely that she has obtained absolute sway over the husband who once loved me, nay, loves me still, were he but free from the fascinations of that beautiful witch. And Zouroff can force Boris from the throne when he chooses."

"He has some secret hold over your husband the Prince?"

"He has. I had better be perfectly frank with you. You remember the abortive attempt ten years ago to federate this peninsula into one kingdom. The Powers deposed no fewer than three princes over that. The scheme was Zouroff's, acting in the interest of Russia. And Zouroff has documentary evidence that Boris was one of the malcontents. Therefore you see how slender is our grasp of our position. Day by day the influence of Boris wanes, day by day is Zouroff stirring up the party of revolution. And to-morrow night everything is arranged for a coup d'etat. If I can force the hand of my enemy, if I can show him degraded and bound to the mob in front of the palace windows, Contigua is saved, and your mission is simultaneously accomplished. That is why I came to you—because I could trust you, and you know the ways of my people. They love me yet, they would do anything at my bidding. At the same time they are like sheep without a shepherd. Will you help me?"

The Princess extended two trembling hands to Moore. He took them in his and raised them to his lips.

"It is both my duty and my inclination to do so," he said. "But I see that you have some plan ready formed in your mind. If you will honor me with your confidence, I shall esteem it a great favor."

The Princess spoke clearly and rapidly. Moore listened with interest and admiration. The plot was one that appealed directly to his imagination. It was dashing, and bold to the last degree. A lurid light shone in his eyes, his pale cheeks were aglow with an unwonted flare.

A pair of rusty, lopsided horses pounded over the cobble-stones of Tenedos in the darkness and pulled up, sobbing, at length before the chief hotel in the town. Moore found that his rooms were all ready for him.

"His Excellency would like supper and lights?" a waiter suggested.

"A light in the bedroom," said Moore, "but the sitting-room can remain in darkness. 1 require no supper; leave me alone. If I want anything I will ring."

Late as it was there were many people still astir. A spirit of unrest seemed to be in the air; there came no sound of mirth from the dull alleys below, nothing more than growls and murmurs, and more than once a subdued murmur of strife hidden by the darkness.

These people were ready for the fray. They only wanted someone to lead them on whether to peace or war mattered little. Moore knew the signs far too well to be mistaken.

With a sudden desire to learn more, he threw a heavy cloak about his shoulders, drew his hat down over his eyes, and plunged into the warm, vaporous gloom of the streets. He passed groups of men standing on the pavements, all of them engaged in a deep discussion of the situation.

From the deeper purple shadow of a minaret Moore paused to listen.

"Boris is not the man he used to be," said one. "Contigua will never be contented so long as Zouroff remains where he is."

"Say Madame Zouroff, rather," sneered another. "She is the cause of all this strife. They say the Prince is infatuated about her. She coveted the diadem belonging to the Princess, and he gave it her. I have it from Marie, the tiring-maid, who is own cousin to my wife. They will be giving Contigua to this Russian adventuress yet."

"Better put the old tiger from the hills on the throne," suggested another.

"No, no," said a third. "Old Taraz is all very well, but he is acting on the side of Russia over those smuggled rifles. Don't you know that Zouroff is plotting to clear the way for Taraz?"

All this palpitated with interest for Moore. That Contigua was seething with intrigue and plot and passion he knew perfectly well. And he knew also that Zouroff regarded Taraz as his creature and tool, whilst the latter was playing false with the man who was helping him on to the little toy throne. The wily old wolf from the hills meant to murder Zouroff without scruple directly his insurrection had proved successful.

All this Moore guessed, and a great deal besides. He was perfectly aware of the fact that the Contigeans for the most part preferred Taraz, for the simple reason that they would rather have the Hillman than the Russian.

The Court and the State were both so small that every bit of gossip and scandal that leaked out was eagerly and greedily lapped up by the people of Tenedos. The affair of the diamond tiara had afforded a toothsome dish for some few days now. And little did these inconsequent babblers realise what an important factor in the history of Contigua the gaud was destined to be.

"To-morrow will prove many things," the first man in the street observed sapiently.

"They say the signal is to be given to-morrow night from the gates of the palace, and then Taraz takes the place of Boris. There will be no riot and no bloodshed."

"There will be both before Taraz's leopards usurp the sway," a big man in a heavy cloak growled. "Had I my way, Zouroff would not live an hour. They say that he carries on his person evidences of his perfidy. If Prince Boris only dared to say the word, all Tenedos would rally to his side and tear the Russian limb from limb. What has come to our ruler I cannot think. What a man he used to be!"

The first speaker gave a heavy sigh.

"It is the old story," he said. "And there is always a woman at the bottom of it. The poor fool is bewitched by Madame Zouroff."

"Who used to be in the chorus of the Bucharest Theatre. An adventuress! A woman whom her sisters would pass by with their skirts drawn aside if they only dared! And we are all puppets who dance when she pulls the strings. Why does not the Princess call upon us? She knows that we are ready to do anything for her. Who'll strike a blow with me?"

None responded, for all were fearful of the shadows and the spies that might lurk therein.

All this was as wine to the listener. This feeling of discontent overlaying a sterling vein of loyalty inspired him. Moore's imagination was inflamed. In his mind's eye he could see himself leading these wild people on to liberty. Then his sense of humor came uppermost, and he smiled. A slight, pale-faced man in pince-nez at the head of this melodramatic mob seemed absurd.

The feeling, the air of discontent, still hovered like a cloud over the capital as Moore drove to the palace the next morning. Prince Boris was pleased to receive the Englishman cordially. His dark, sensitive face showed power and ambition, though the mouth was a trifle weak and sensual. And Prince Boris was not alone.

With him was a tall, slim man with a clean-shaven face and a pair of eyes that gleamed with evil black fires. A sneer was on his face as he bowed to the stranger. Moore had no need to be told who this man was.

"I can guess your errand," Zouroff remarked in sleek, purring tones, "and you will find us ready to give you every assistance. The air of Tenedos seems to be bad for you Englishmen. But then you are so adventurous."

A distinct threat underlay these last few words. A desire to fly at the throat of the speaker filled Moore. Under Zouroff's close fitting frock-coat lay goodness knows how many secrets, the documentary evidence Moore would have given years to possess. For Zouroff was a stormy petrel of intrigue and was far too cunning to be parted from that knowledge and proof of it which was power to him. Any trick of Fortune might render him outcast again; at any moment he might have to fly. For that reason he carried his secrets on his person.

"You have gauged our character correctly, sir," Moore responded. "The idiosyncrasy you speak of is the one trait that has made England great. When we undertake a thing, at any cost we succeed."

Zouroff took up the challenge lightly.

"We shall see," he responded. "As I said before, the climate is not a healthy one. If you can see a way to remedy that—"

"There is such a thing as removing the source of the pestilence."

Zouroff smiled no more. On the contrary he looked troubled. It began to come to him that here was an antagonist worthy of his steel.

Prince Boris looked on uneasily. Polite as he might be to Zouroff, he would have given his right hand to be freed from his chief adviser, the man who played him as a puppet and dangled the terror of the Powers before his eyes.

"You must not heed all my friend Zouroff says," he interpolated. "He is one who has reduced badinage to a fine art. He is not to be taken seriously."

"On the contrary, your Highness," Moore replied, "I imagine that there are times when it behoves the wise man to take M. Zouroff very seriously indeed!"

"You will dine with us at seven to-night?" the Prince asked abruptly.

Moore had been waiting for the invitation which he knew perfectly well was coming. It tickled his vanity a little to know that a counter-plot was being worked out under the nose of the arch-conspirator, Zouroff.

"I shall be only too pleased and honored," Moore replied.

At the same moment another man entered the room. He was an old man with eagle-like features. He had the fighting light in his eyes and the free swing of the hills in his brown limbs. His white flowing robes sat with wondrous grace on his powerful frame. Despite his deference, his mien was not devoid of cool insolence.

"This is Taraz of the Hills," Prince Boris said briefly. "You will meet again to-night."

Taraz deigned no glance for Moore. His Oriental hauteur was perfect. Seeing that the interview was ended, Moore turned to go. As he passed into the wide flagged corridor Zouroff followed him.

Moore turned his eyes full upon the face of the Russian.

"I will take your advice," he said, "and leave Tenedos—to-morrow!"

Moore dressed himself with scrupulous care for his part. Ostensibly he was a quiet-looking gentleman in evening dress, who was going out to dinner. As a matter of fact, he was playing a leading part in a tragedy wherein he might essay the role of the murdered hero or save Europe from a conflagration according to the whim of Dame Fate, sole spectator of the drama.

As a trusted servant of the Secret Service, the Service whose doings even the inquisitive M.P. has no right to question, Moore had been in danger before, but never in such deadly peril as this.

Zouroff meant to murder him. Zouroff knew what he was doing here. To check-mate the Russian, to stop the inflow of rifles, and to free Prince Boris from this old man of the sea was Moore's business here.

"Heaven be praised that I have a bold woman on my side," he muttered. "Within the next two hours the matter will be decided one way or another. A pity that Princess Natalie has nobody here she can really trust but me. And yet, if she succeeds, all Contigua will be at her feet to- morrow."

Moore gave the last finishing touches to his toilette, and rang the bell for the carriage.

"You will have the supper I have ordered ready for me at midnight," he remarked. "If I am not here by then the meal will not be required."

Practically Moore had eaten nothing for twenty-four hours. The mere thought of food filled him with a sense of nausea, though under ordinary circumstances his appetite was normal. However dainty the meal at the palace might be, Moore knew that he would touch none of it.

Vivid and agitated as was Moore's imagination, it did not blind him to the disturbed state of the streets as he drove along. Knots of men were gathered together eagerly discussing the state of affairs, and for the nonce the women were swept back to the shelter of the homesteads. In the Palace Square hundreds of people were loitering as if waiting for something.

They seemed moody and discontented rather than openly rebellious. They had the air of men who were prepared to follow one leader, provided they could not get another one that they liked better.

"It will be touch and go," Moore murmured. "If the Princess is successful, Contigua and the situation are both saved."

Meanwhile inside the palace the note was one of comedy. In a pillared hall, carved and fretted, and ornamented with painted panels and figures in armor, Prince Boris and his consort were receiving their guests. For the most part, indeed, with the solitary exception of Taraz, they were all dressed in the stereotyped Western mould, and the whole party numbered exactly twelve.

Moore presently found himself vaguely made known to all of them. But there was no interest for him there beyond the Prince and Princess, Taraz, and Zouroff, and last, but by no means least, the brilliant adventuress whom Zouroff called his wife.

A slight, fair woman, with a dazzling smile and teeth. In the red lips and deep blue eyes, Moore recognised the diabolical beauty of de L'Enclos, that power over men that fascinated them and drove them mad. There was something cruel about such loveliness. The ivory whiteness of the woman's shoulders was concealed as yet, for the salon was chilly, and Madame Zouroff had a filmy wrap around her.

From time to time she glanced in the direction of the Princess, and then Moore saw plainly the full treachery of that flashing smile. Nothing was lost to the eyes of the man who was a novelist as well as a man of action.

Conversation proceeded fitfully, for the Prince appeared uneasy and distrait, and the Princess maintained a stern silence. Her face was white and waxen as the camellias at her breast, her eyes glowed with a steadfast fire.

"She looks like a leopard in a cage," Madame Zouroff whispered to her husband.

"Exactly what she is," the Russian answered carelessly. "Natalie is a clever woman, and one who knows when she is beaten; and I shall find the means to tame her before the evening is over."

"The people are uneasy, you think?"

"I am certain of it. I have successfully alienated them from their Prince. Any leader is better than none, and Taraz is preferable to Russia. If they only knew that they are synonymous! But they don't. If you listen carefully you can hear the murmur of the crowd in the Square."

Madame smiled as her little pink ears caught the distant murmur. It was like the rise of an angry tide.

A servant in livery threw back the folding-doors with the announcement that dinner was served. Moore caught the eye of Princess Natalie as she passed him, and the look she gave him braced his courage.

The man of action was himself now. The dread of the unknown, the unforeseen, had passed out of him in the presence of the fray. He felt a buoyant sense of triumph, saw luminous visions of success.

For some time the dinner proceeded in silence. Then, as the wine loosened the tongues of the guests, something like gaiety prevailed. Alert, vigorous, catlike, Moore glanced round the table. Nothing escaped his lightning glance.

The hour was approaching. Outside the murmur of voices grew louder, even so as to intrude upon the conversation of the dinner-table. Some rude orator was apparently addressing the mob. A scornful smile flitted over Princess Natalie's face.

"These Western ideas of popular liberty are contagious," she said.

In the light of the one solitary lamp on the dinner-table the features of the speaker were more waxlike than before. As to the rest of the room, it was in total darkness. In the shadows the liveried servants were flitting around.

"Prince Boris had much to answer for," Zouroff smiled.

"And you are doubtless blameless?" Natalie asked.

The question was a challenge. Conversation went out like a falling star. Natalie rose and ordered the servants from the room. With a loud snap she turned the key in the lock. A shudder of excitement ran round the room. With a little smile Madame Zouroff threw back her wrap and reclined in her chair.

"You must be strong to speak to me thus," Zouroff said hoarsely.

Moore was watching the speaker intently. He sat but one chair removed, and the Englishman seemed to be carefully measuring the distance between them with his eye. On Natalie's right hand was Taraz, grave and immovable as the carved eagle on a lectern. The eyes of the Princess were blazing; the thin veneer of civilisation had peeled off.

"I am stronger than you imagine," she cried.

Madame Zouroff laughed. Natalie turned upon her furiously.

"You shameless creature," she cried. "You steal my husband's love from me, you boast of it in the market-place. And in your hair and on your breast you wear the jewels that are mine. He gave them you, and you dare flaunt them before me."

"And you dare malign my wife's name!" Zouroff cried.

"Your wife is too vicious to be anything but virtuous," Natalie retorted. "I do not blame the Prince. I know that once the fascination is removed, he will be a man again. And it is going to be removed to-night. Give me those jewels."

The haughty command swept Madame Zouroff almost off her feet for the moment. She made an involuntary movement to her breast.

"No, no," Zouroff shouted. "It shall not be."

"And I say it shall. It shall, it shall, and now."

As Natalie uttered the last word with a scream she rose to her feet and reached across the table. As she did so Moore noticed that The hilt of a dagger gleamed in her corsage. Then he turned his eyes again to Zouroff.

The next instant the lamp upon the table went crashing over and expired, leaving the whole room in intense darkness, save for a tiny pool of vaporous blue flame upon the fair white damask. With a cry most of the guests made for the door, only to find the key in the lock missing.

A thin hysterical chuckle broke from Moore's lips. His brain was aflame, and his fingers were tingling for action, for the time had come at last.

No sooner had the lamp gone over than he literally dived for Zouroff. Up to now the whole thing had fallen out exactly as he and Natalie had planned. The room was in intense darkness, the rest of the frightened guests were huddled up near the door; there was no chance of interruption. And upon Zouroff's person were papers worth a king's ransom.

Moore landed fairly on the neck of his antagonist. With delirious joy he clutched the Russian by the throat and bore him to the ground. All Moore's sinewy strength and agility were exerted. He was fighting for the success of his mission, he was fighting for his own life, and to avenge the three good men who had gone before him.

Zouroff was no stripling, and no coward to boot, but he had been utterly taken by surprise. He was in the grip of a man who was quite prepared to strangle him if necessary; he knew that he was fighting for his days in the land.

But that grip was not to be shaken off, it held on till the great red lights filled the Russian's eyes and the sound of the sea roared in his ears. Zouroff dropped, dropped into the tepid waters of oblivion. He felt ghostly hands seeking in his pockets, a heaping rush of the warm red tide, and then unconsciousness.

Moore had the papers. He drew from his hip pocket a slender pair of handcuffs and snapped them on the wrists of the Russian. At the same moment a frightened mob of servants burst open the doors, throwing back the windows so that the room might have the benefit of the light from the Square. The blast of air caught the blue vapor on the dinner table, and set it all in a great yellow blaze.

There was light enough now with a vengeance. Only five people remained. On the floor, with a dagger in his heart, lay Taraz, stone dead. The features were calm and placid, for a death mercifully swift had overtaken him.

The flames rose higher and higher. Down below in the Square some hundreds of people were packed, hot, eager, impetuous Already something of the truth had flashed like wildfire across the black mass. As Zouroff staggered to his feet the Princess caught him by the arm, and dragged him, dazed and blind and staggering with weakness, out on the balcony.

The lurid light behind lit up the two figures. There was one long hoarse roar from the human wolves below, and then a silence almost painful in its grim, clinging intensity. For the people there knew what had happened as if they had seen the tragedy of the darkness.

An hour later and Tenedos was all aflare with torches. For Taraz was no more, and Zouroff lay where he was incapable of further mischief. His power was broken, the weapons he relied upon were in Moore's possession. And every man in the yelling mob was aflame with patriotism and reeking with the fumes of madness inspired by Natalie's proclamation from the balcony with the flashing flames behind her.

"Are you satisfied?" she asked Newton Moore. "Are you sure you have succeeded?"

"I have nothing more to desire," said Moore. "and I am not disposed to ask any awkward questions. But for you I should have failed. You certainly seemed to understand the psychological moment. And if this thing can only be kept out of the European papers—"

Princess Natalie smiled significantly.

THE MAZAROFF RIFLE

Newton Moore came into the War Office in response to a code telegram and a hint that speed was the essence of the contract. Sir George Morley plunged immediately into his subject.

"I've got a pretty case for you," he said. "I suppose you have never heard of such a thing as the Mazaroff rifle?"

Moore admitted his ignorance. He opined that it was something new, and that something had gone wrong with the lethal weapon in question.

"Quite right, and it will be your business to recover it," Sir George explained. "The gun is the invention of a clever young Russian, Nicholas Mazaroff by name. We have tested the weapon, which, as a matter of fact, we have purchased from Mazaroff. The rifle is destined to entirely revolutionise infantry tactics, and, indeed, it is a most wonderful affair. The projectile is fired by liquid air, there are no cartridges, and, as there is practically no friction beyond the passage of the bullet from the barrel, it is possible to fire the rifle some four hundred times before recharging. In addition, there is absolutely no smoke and no noise. You can imagine the value of the discovery."

"I can indeed," Moore observed. "I should very much like to see it."

"And I should like you to see it of all things," Sir George said drily; "indeed, I hope you will be the very first to see it, considering that the gun and its sectional plans have been stolen."

Newton Moore smiled. He knew now why he had been sent for.

"Stolen from here, Sir George?" he asked.

"Stolen from here yesterday afternoon by means of a trick. Mazaroff called to see me, but I was very busy. Then he asked to see my assistant, Colonel Parkinson. He seemed to be in considerable trouble, so Parkinson told me. He had discovered a flaw in his rifle, a tendency for the projectile to jam, which constituted a danger to the marksman. Could he have the rifle and the plans for a day or two, he asked? Naturally, there was no objection to this, and the boon was granted. Mazaroff came here an hour ago, and when I asked him if he had remedied the defect, he paralysed me by declaring that he knew nothing whatever about the caller yesterday; indeed, he is prepared to prove that he was in Liverpool till a late hour last night. Some clever rascal impersonated him and got clear away with the booty."

"I presume Colonel Parkinson knew Mazaroff?"

"Not very well, but well enough to have no doubt as to his identity. Naturally, Parkinson is fearfully upset over the business; indeed, he seems to fancy that Mazaroff is lying to us. Mazaroff generally comes here in a queer, old Inverness cloak, with ragged braid, and a shovel hat with a brown stain on the left side. Parkinson swears that he noticed both these things yesterday."

"I should like to see Mazaroff," Moore replied.

Sir George touched a bell, and from an inner room a young man, with a high, broad forehead, and dark, restless eyes, emerged. He was badly dressed, and, sooth to say, not over clean. Newton Moore's half-shy glance took him in from head to foot with the swiftness of a snapshot.

"This is the Russian gentleman I spoke of," said Sir George. "Mr. Newton Moore."

"Russian only in name," said Mazaroff swiftly. "I am English. If you help me to get my gun back I shall never be sufficiently grateful."

"I am going to have a good try," Moore replied. "Meanwhile, I shall require your undivided attention for some little time. I should like to walk with you as far as your lodgings and have a chat with you there."

Moore had made up his mind as to his man. He felt perfectly convinced that he was speaking the truth. He piloted Mazaroff into the street, and then took his arm.

"I am going to get you to conduct me to your rooms," he said. "And I am going to ask you a prodigious lot of questions. First, and most important—does anyone, to your knowledge, know of the new rifle?"

"Not a soul; I had a friend, a partner two years ago, who saw the thing nearly complete, but he is dead."

"Your partner might have mentioned the matter to somebody else."

"He might. Poor Franz was of a convivial nature. He did not possess the real secret."

"No, but he might have hinted to somebody that you were on the verge of a gigantic discovery. That somebody might have kept his eye upon you; he might have seen you coming from and going into the War Office."

Mazaroff nodded gravely. All these things were on the knees of the gods.

"At any rate somebody must have known, and somebody must have impersonated you," Moore proceeded. "You haven't a notion who it was, so I will not bother you any further in that direction. I have to look for a cool and clever scoundrel, and one, moreover, who is a consummate actor."

"Cool enough," Mazaroff said drily, "seeing that the fellow actually had the impudence to pass himself off on my landlady as myself, and borrow my hat and Inverness—the ones I am wearing now—and cool enough to return them."

All this Mazaroff's landlady subsequently confirmed. She had known, of course, that her lodger had gone to Liverpool on business, and she had been surprised to see him return. The alter ego had muttered something about being suddenly recalled; he had taken off a frock coat and tall hat similar to those Mazaroff had used to travel in, and he had gone out immediately with the older and more familar garments.

"You had no suspicions?" Moore asked. The landlady was fat, but by no means scant of breath. It was the misfortune of a lady who had fallen from high social status that she was compelled to inhabit a house of considerable gloom. Furthermore, her eyes were not the limpid orbs into which many lovers had once looked languishingly. Was a body to blame when slippery rascals were about?

"Nobody is blaming a body," Newton Moore smiled. "I don't think we need trouble you any more, Mrs. Jarrett."

Mrs. Jarrett departed with an avowed resolution to "have the law" of somebody or other over this business, and a blissful silence followed. Mazaroff had stripped off his hat and coat.

"You must have been carefully watched yesterday," Moore observed. "I suppose this is the hat and cloak your double borrowed?"

Mazaroff nodded, and Moore proceeded to examine the cloak. It was just possible that the thief might have left some clue, however small. Moore turned out the pockets.

"I am certain you will find nothing there," said Mazaroff. "There is a hole in both pockets, and I am careful to carry nothing in them."

"Nothing small, I suppose you mean," Moore replied as he brought to light some dingy looking papers folded like a brief. He threw the bundle on the table, and Mazaroff proceeded to examine it languidly. A puzzled look came over his face.

"These are not mine," he declared. "I never saw them before."

There were some score or more sheets fastened together with a brass stud. The sheets were typed, the letter-press was in the form of a dialogue. In fact the whole formed a play-part from some comedy or drama.

"This is a most important discovery," Moore observed. "Our friend must have been studying this on his way along and forgot it finally. We know now what I have suspected all along—that the man who impersonated you was by profession an actor. That is something gained."

Mazaroff caught a little of his companion's excitement.

"You can go farther," he cried. "You can find who this belongs to."

"Precisely what I am going to do," said Moore. "It is a fair inference that our man is playing in a new comedy or is taking the part of somebody else at short notice, or he could not have been learning this up in the cab. I have a friend who is an inveterate theatre-goer, a man who has a pecuniary interest in a number of playhouses, and I am in hopes that he may be able to locate this part for me. I'll see him at once."

Moore drove away without further delay to Ebury Street, where dwelt the Honourable Jimmy Manningtree, an old young man with a strong taste for the drama, and a good notion of getting value for the money he was fond of investing therein. He was an apple-faced individual with a keen eye and a marvellous memory for everything connected with the stage.

"Bet you I'll fit that dialogue to the play like a shot," he said when Moore had explained his errand. "Have some breakfast?"

Moore declined. Until he had identified his man, food was a physical impossibility. Hungry as he was he felt that the first mouthful would choke him. He took up a cigarette and lay back in a chair whilst Manningtree pondered over the type-written sheets before him.

"Told you I'd name the lady," he cried presently. "I don't propose to identify and give the precise name of the character, because you'll be able to do that for yourself by following the play carefully."

"But what is the name of the play? "Moore asked impatiently.

"It is called 'Noughts and Crosses,' one of the most popular comedies we have ever run at the Thespian. If you weren't so buried in your stories and your medicine mysteries at the War Office, you might have seen all about it in last Monday's papers. Go and see the show—I'll give you a box."

"Then the play was produced for the first time on Saturday night," Moore was panting and eager on the scent at last. "Also, from what you say, the Thespian is one of the theatres you are interested in?"

Manningtree executed a wink of amazing slyness. The Honourable Jimmy was no mean comedian himself.

"I believe you, my boy," he said. "I've got ten thousand locked up there, and I shall get it back three times over out of 'Noughts and Crosses.' If you like to have a box to-night you can."

"You're very kind," Moore replied. He laid his hands across his knees to steady them. "And, as much always wants more, I shall be greatly obliged if you will give me the run of the theatre. In other words, can I come behind?"

"Well, I don't encourage that kind of thing as a rule," Manningtree replied, "but as I know you have some strong reason for the request, I'll make an exception in your favour. I don't run my show for marbles, dear boy. I shall be at the Thespian at ten, and then, if you send round your card, the thing is done. Only I should like to know what you are driving at."

Moore smiled quietly.

"I dare say you would," he said. "Later on perhaps. For the present my lips are sealed. No breakfast, thanks—I couldn't swallow a mouthful. Only don't fail me tonight as you love your country."

A brilliant audience filled the Thespian. The stalls were one flash of colour and glitter of gems. The comedy was lively and sparkling, there was a strong story on which the jewels were threaded.

From the corner of his box Moore followed the progress of the play.

The first act was nearing its close. There were two characters in the caste still unaccounted for, and one of these must of necessity be the man Moore was after. The crux of the act was approaching. A thin, dark man stood on the stage. In style and carriage he had a marked resemblance to Mazaroff. He came to the centre of the stage and laid a hand on the shoulder of the high comedy man there.

"And where do I come in?" he asked gently.

It was a quotation, the first line of the play-part spread out on the ledge of the box before Moore. He gave a gasp. He saw a chance here that he determined to take. As the curtain fell on the second act he sent round his card. A little later and he was in Manningtree's private room.

"Who is the man playing the part of Paul Gilroy?" he asked.

"Oh, come," Manningtree protested. "You're not going to deprive me of Hermann. He has made the piece."

"I am going to do nothing of the kind," Moore replied. "We don't make public anything we can possibly keep to ourselves. Only Hermann has some information I require, and there is only one way of getting it. Tell me all you know about that man."

"Well, in the first place, he is a German with an American mother. He seems to have been everything, from a police spy up to a University Fellow. He speaks four or five languages fluently. A shady sort of a chap, but a brilliant actor, as you are bound to admit. Wait till you see him in the last act."

"He has all what you call the 'fat,' I presume?"

"He is on the stage the whole time. Five-and-twenty minutes the act plays. Take my advice and don't miss a word of it."

"I am afraid I shall miss it all," Moore replied in a dropping voice. "I am afraid that I shall be compelled to wander into Mr. Hermann's dressing-room by mistake. In an absent-minded kind of way I may also go through his pockets. Don't protest, there's a good fellow. You know me sufficiently well to be certain that I am acting in high interests. Say nothing, but merely let me know which is my man's dressing-room."

"You're a rum chap," Manningtree grumbled, "but you always manage to get your own way. You are running a grave risk, but you will have to take the consequences. If you are caught I cannot save you."

"I won't ask you to," Moore replied.

Manningtree indicated the room and strolled away. The room was empty. Hermann's dresser had disappeared, knowing probably that his services would not be required for the next half-hour. There was a quick tinkle of the bell, and the curtain drew up on the last act. Moore from his dim corner heard Hermann "called," and the coast was clear at last.

Just for a moment Moore hesitated. He had literally to force himself forward, but once the door had closed behind him his courage returned.

Hermann's ordinary clothing first. It hung up on the door. For some time Moore could find nothing of the least value, to him at any rate. He came at length to a pocket-book, which he opened without ceremony. There were papers and private letters, but nothing calculated to give a clue. In one of the flaps of the pocket a card, an ordinary visiting-card, had been stuck. It bore the name of Emile Nobel.

Moore fairly danced across the floor. He hustled the pocket-book back in its place and flashed out of the room. Nobody was near, nobody heard his chuckle. The whole atmosphere trembled with applause, applause that Moore in his strange way took to himself. He had solved the problem.

The name on the card was one perfectly well known to him. Every tyro in the employ of the Secret Service Fund had heard of Emile Nobel. For he was perhaps the chief rascal in the Rogues' Gallery of Europe. Newton Moore knew him both by name and by sight.

Stolen dispatches, purloined plans, nothing came amiss to the great, gross German, who seemed to have been at the bottom of half the mischief which it was the business of the Secret Service to set right. Moore had never come in actual contact with Nobel before, but he felt pretty sure that he was going to do so on this occasion. He was dealing with a clever coward, a man stone deaf, strange to say, but a man of infinite resources and cunning. Added to all this, Nobel was a chemist of great repute. The Secret Service heard vague legends of mysterious murders done by Nobel, all strictly in the way of business. And Nobel had this gun—Moore felt certain of that. Hermann had accomplished the theft, doubtless for a substantial pecuniary consideration. Nobel must be found.

Moore saw his way clearly directly. It was a mere game of chance. If Hermann really knew Nobel—and the possession of the latter's visiting-card seemed to prove it—the thing might be easily accomplished. If not, then no harm would be done.

Moore made his way rapidly past the dark little box by the stage-door into the street. Then he whistled softly. A figure emerged from the gloom of the court.

"You called me, sir," a voice whispered.

"I did, Joseph," Moore replied. "One little thing and you can retire for to-night. Take this card. In a few minutes you are to present it—as your own, mind— to the keeper of the stage-door yonder. Take care that the door-keeper does not see your face, and address him in fair English with a strong German accent. You will ask to see Mr. Hermann, and the stage-door keeper will inform you that you cannot see him for some time. You are to say that you are stone deaf, and get him to write what he says on paper. Then you leave your card for Mr. Hermann saying that you must see him on most important business to-night. Will he be good enough to come round and see you? That is all, Joseph."

Then Moore slipped back into the theatre. He had the satisfaction of hearing the message given, and his instructions carried out without a hitch. And a little later on he had the further satisfaction of hearing the stage-door keeper carry out Joseph's instructions as far as Hermann was concerned. Had Nobel's address been on the card all this would have been superfluous. As the address was missing, the little scheme was absolutely necessary.

There was just a chance, of course, that Hermann might deny all knowledge of Moore's prospective quarry, not that Moore had much fear of this, after the episode of the borrowed cloak and the play-part. Hermann stood flushed and smiling as he received the compliments of fellow comedians. Moore watched him keenly as the stage-door keeper delivered the card and the message.

"Most extraordinary," Hermann muttered. "You say that Mr. Nobel was here himself. What was he like?"

"Big gentleman, sir, strong foreign accent and deaf as a post."

Hermann looked relieved, but the puzzled expression was still on his face.

"All right, Blotton," he said. "Send somebody out to call a cab for me in ten minutes. Sorry I can't come and sup with you fellows as arranged. A matter of business has suddenly cropped up."

Moore left the theatre without further delay. His little scheme had worked like a charm. All lay clear before him now. Hermann had important business with Nobel, he knew where the latter was staying, he was going unceremoniously to conduct Moore to his abode. And where Nobel was at present there was the Mazaroff rifle. There could be no doubt about that now. Naturally the upshot of all this would be that both the conspirators would discover that someone was on the trail, but Moore could see no way of getting the desired information without alarming the enemy. Once he knew where to look for the thimble he felt that the search would be easy. Also he was prepared for a bold and audacious stroke if necessary.

With his vivid and delicate fancy, it was only the terrors conjured up by his own marvellous imagination that terrified him. He was one bundle of quivering nerves, and the power of the cigarettes he practically lived on jangled the machine more terribly out of tune.

But there was a sense of exultation now; the mad, feline courage Moore always felt when his clear, shrewd brain was shaping to success. At moments like these he was capable of the most amazing courage. He had a presentiment that success lay broadly before him.

A cab crawled along the dingy street at the mouth of the court, leading to the stage-door of the Thespian. Moore hailed it and got in.

"Don't move till I give you the signal," said he, "and keep the trap open."

The cabman grinned and chuckled. This was evidently going to be one of the class of fares that London's gondoliers dream of but so seldom see. Presently the cab bearing Hermann away shot past.

"Follow that," Moore cried, "and when the gentleman gets out slacken speed, but on no account stop. I will drop out of the cab when it is still moving. There is a sovereign for you in any case, and there is my card in case I should have a very long journey. Now push her along."

It was a long journey. Neither cab boasted horse-flesh of high calibre, and after a time the pursuit dawdled down to a funeral procession.

Near the flagstaff at Hampstead Heath the first cab stopped and Hermann descended. Moore's cab trotted by, but Moore was no longer inside. If Hermann had any suspicion of being followed, it was allayed by this neat stroke of Moore's.

Hermann hurried forward, walking for half an hour until he came to a long new road at the foot of the hill between Cricklewood and Hampstead. Only one of the fairly large houses there seemed to be inhabited, the rest were in the last stages of completion. The opposite side of the road was an open field.

The houses were double-fronted ones with a large porch and entrance hall, and a long strip of lawn in front. Hermann paused before the house which appeared to be inhabited, and passing up the path opened the front door and entered, closing the big door behind him. In the room on the left-hand side of the hall a brilliant light gleamed, but no glimmer showed in the hall itself. Beyond a doubt Emile Nobel was here.

Moore followed cautiously along the drive. He softly tried the front door, only to find the key had been turned in the lock.

"They are alarmed," he muttered; "the covey has been disturbed. By this time Nobel and Hermann know that they have been hoaxed. Also they will have a pretty good idea why. If I am any judge of character, audacity more than pluck is Hermann's strong point. He will leave Nobel in the lurch as soon as possible. If I could only hear what is going on! But that is impossible."

Moore could hear nothing beyond the murmur of Nobel's heavy voice, Hermann of course responding with signals. For a long time this continued.

Meanwhile Moore was not altogether idle. He had marked Hermann's unsteady eye and the weakness of his mouth. He sized him up as a man who would have scant consideration for others where his own personal safety was concerned.

"Anyway I'm going on that line," Moore muttered. "If Hermann discovers that he has been hoaxed without betraying his knowledge to Nobel, he will be certain to say nothing to him, but will as certainly abandon him to his fate. Nobel's deafness will be an important factor in this direction. Hermann's walking into the house as he did seems to indicate the absence of servants here. That will be in my favour later on. Doubtless Nobel has taken this house as a blind—much safer than rooms in London, anyway. There is probably little or no furniture here, so that Nobel can slip off at any time. And now to see if I can find some way of getting into the house."

Whilst Moore was working away steadily with a stiff clasp-knife at a loose catch in one of the panes of the hall window, a conversation much on the lines Moore had indicated was taking place inside.

The hall was comfortably furnished, as was also the one sitting-room, where the brilliant light was burning. Over a table littered with plans and drawings a ponderous German was bending. He had a huge head, practically bald, a great red face, and cold blue eyes, and his mouth was the mouth of a shark. There was no air of courage or resolution about him, but a suggestion of diabolical cunning. A more brilliant rascal Europe could not boast.

Nobel looked up with a start as Hermann touched him.

"You frightened me," he said. "My nerfs are not as gombletely under gontrol as they might be. Is anything wrong, my tear friendt?"

"Wrong? "Hermann cried. "Why, you sent for me."

Nobel shook his head, for he had not heard a word.

"I was goming to see you to-morrow," he said. "I should have come to-night, but you were engaged at the theatre. Eh, what?"

Hermann turned away to light a cigarette. His hands shook and his knees trembled under him. He had been hoaxed; in a flash he saw his danger before him. Perhaps he had been tracked and followed here. And Nobel knew nothing of it. He was not going to know, either, if his accomplice could help it.

"I came to warn you," he touched off on his fingers.

"Oh," Nobel cried, "there is tanger, then? You have heard something?"

Hermann proceeded to telegraph a negative reply. He had seen nothing whatever; only the last few hours he had a strong suspicion of being followed. He discreetly omitted to remark the absolute conviction that he had been shadowed this evening. He had deemed it his solemn duty to come and warn Nobel, seeing what compromising matter the latter had in his house.

"You are a goot boy," Nobel said, patting Hermann ponderously on the shoulder. "By the morning I shall have gomitted all the plans of that weapon to my brain. Then I will destroy him and the plans. After, I go to Paris, and you shall hear from me there. Meanwhile there is branty and whiskey."

Hermann signalled that he would take nothing. It was of first importance that he should return to London without delay. He had come down there at great inconvenience to himself. As a matter of fact every sound in the empty house set his nerves going like a set of cracked bells. Moore had only just time to plunge into the darkness as the front door opened and Hermann came out. Moore smiled grimly as he heard the lock turned, and saw Hermann hurrying away.

Things had fallen out exactly as he had anticipated. Hermann had told his big confederate nothing. He meant to abandon him to his fate. Nobel was in the house, where he meant to remain for the present. Hermann had given him no cause for alarm.

It was going to be a case of man to man; brains and agility against cunning. Doubtless Nobel was not unprepared for an attack. There would be nothing so clumsy as mere fire-arms—there were other and more terrible weapons known to the German, who was a chemist and a scientist of a high order.

But the thing had to be done and Moore meant to do it. There was no need for silence. He worked away at the window catch, which presently flew back with a click and the sash was opened. A moment later and Moore was in the hall. As he dropped lightly to his feet it seemed to his quick ear that a deep suppressed growl followed. There was darkness in the hall with just one shaft of light crossing it from the room beyond, where Moore could distinctly see Nobel bending over a table. The low growl was repeated. As Moore peered into the darkness he saw two round spots of flaming angry orange, two balls of flame close together near the floor. He gave a startled cry that rang in the house, then paused as if half fearful of disturbing Nobel. But the latter never moved. He would never hear again till the last trumpet sounded.

The flaming circles crept nearer to Moore. He did not dare to turn and fly. He saw the gleaming eyes describe an arc, and then next moment he was on his back on the floor, with the bulldog uppermost.

A fierce flash of two rows of gleaming teeth were followed by a stinging blow on the temple, from which the blood flowed freely. Then the dog's grip met in the thick, fleshy part of the shoulder. As the cruel saws gashed on Moore's collar-bone he felt faint and sick with the pain.

But he uttered no further cry; he knew how useless it was. There was something peculiarly horrible in the idea of lying there in sight of help and yet being totally unable to invoke it.

Moore's hand went up to his tie slowly. From it he withdrew a diamond pin, the shaft of which, as is not uncommon with valuable pins, being made of steel. His hand thus armed, crept under the left forearm of the bulldog, until it rested just over the strongly-beating heart. With a steady pressure Moore drove the pin home to the head.

There was one convulsive snap on Moore's collarbone, then the teeth relaxed. A shudder, a long-drawn sigh, and all was still. Some minutes passed before Moore had strength to recover his feet, A queer, hysterical laugh escaped him as he raised the carcase of the dog in his arms. A sudden strength possessed him, a sudden madness held him. With the dog in his arms, he staggered into the room where Nobel was so deeply engrossed, and flung the carcase with a crash upon the table.

A frightened cry came from Nobel as he staggered back. His great red face grew white and flabby, his blue eyes were filled with tears. He looked from the carcase on the table to the slight man with the blood on his features. On the table lay the object of Moore's search, the Mazaroff rifle.

"A ghost!" Nobel cried. "A ghost! Ah! what does it mean?"

Moore pointed to the rifle and the drawings on the table.

"Those," he signalled upon his fingers.

"I do not understand," he muttered.

"Not now," Moore replied. He was proficient with that code used by the deaf. More than once he had proved its value. "But you hope to understand that rifle before morning. I have come to take it away. You need not trouble to go into explanations. I am perfectly aware how you and Hermann managed the thing between you."

"My servants," Nobel muttered, "will—"

"You have no servants, you are quite alone in the house."

Nobel smiled in a peculiar manner, and, as if to disprove the statement, laid a finger on the electric bell. At the same time he seemed to be caressing his nostrils with a handkerchief. Moore was conscious of a faint, sweet smell in the air, and the next minute a giddy feeling came over him. A terrible smile danced in Nobel's eyes.

Some infernal juggling was at work here. Moore glanced towards the electric bell. Then he saw that the white stud was no longer there— there was nothing but a round hole, through which doubtless some deadly gas was pouring. With a handkerchief held to his face, Moore snatched up the plans from the table and crushed them into the heart of the fire. He gripped the Mazaroff rifle by the barrel, and held it over Nobel's huge head. "You scoundrel," he muttered, "you are trying to murder me. Open the windows, open the windows at once, or I will beat your brains out."

Nobel, understood enough of this from Moore's threatening gesture to know that he had been found out and what was required of him. With his huge, flabby form trembling like a jelly, he pulled up the curtains and opened one of the windows. It was close to the ground, the lawn coming up to the house. In a sudden paroxysm of rage, Moore's left hand shot out, catching Nobel full on the side of his ponderous cheek.

There was an impact of flesh on flesh, and Nobel went down like a magnificent ruin. As he staggered to his feet again he caught a glimpse of a flying figure hurrying at top speed down the road.

"My kingdom for the Edgware Road and a cab," Moore panted. "I'm going to collapse, I'm played out for the present. Thank the gods there is a policeman. Hi, Robert, Robert. Here's a case of drunk and incapable for you. And, whatever happens to me, don't lose my rifle. Give me your arm, don't be too hard upon me, and we shall get to Cricklewood Police Station all in good time."

IN THE EXPRESS

A yellow fog hung over a part of Glasgow. The foul cloudland came to Newton Moore's nostrils, pricked his throat, filled him with a horror he had found it hard to name. His clothes hung limp with moisture as he crouched closer to the wall listening. In the same attitude the famous Secret Service Agent had remained since darkness fell. The cigarette between his teeth had spent itself, and he had no more matches. So he stood trembling there, waiting for the hour when he could strike, and then hasten to the food he had not touched for a score of hours.

It was one of the biggest things Moore had ever been engaged in. If successful, he hoped to lay by the heels the most daring scoundrel in Europe. Not a government was there which had no cause to dread Alex Mefer; no plan or treaty had leaked out these twenty years without Mefer being at the bottom of the business.

For the present, however, Moore's occupation partook more or less of the nature of a side-show. It was a means to an end, a part of a little scheme worked out by him in a drift of cigarette smoke burnt in with the midnight hours.

Now and again a figure drifted by. Then came a step lighter than the rest, and Moore stood up quivering. A tall man passed him, an exceedingly handsome man with a face of bronze, and gold rings in his ears. As this obviously Italian beauty passed on, Moore followed.

He found himself presently ascending a flight of stairs in a building let out in rooms to all and sundry who possessed the desired means to pay for them, a building of philanthropy with a backing of 5 per cent behind it. Into a room on the third floor the Italian entered.

Moore crept after his quarry like a cat. He stood in the open doorway whilst the foreigner lighted his lamp. An instant later the door was closed, and the Italian was lying back in the chair with a grip on his throat and a black terror glazing his eyes.

"Signor Moore," he gurgled, "Signor Moore!"

Moore relaxed his grip. He had established the full measure of fear he had anticipated. That he was dealing with an arrant coward he already knew. Even cowards have their use in the way of Queen's evidence.

"You didn't expect to see me here?" Moore asked. "Eh, Stefano?"

Stefano shook his head sadly. His dark eyes were drawn to Moore with a sort of dazed fascination.

"I am doing no harm," he said sullenly.

"You came from Florence with Tosco and Berthe and—and another one," said Moore. "And Katrina is in the business. I haven't been following up your little lot for the last two months for nothing. I know exactly where those glycerine shells are at present and also what you are going to do with them. Tosco and Berthe will have a pleasant surprise presently."

Stefano's eyes dilated still further.

"In this country," Moore went on, "men who endanger human life by blowing up public buildings and the like seldom escape with less than twenty years' penal servitude. How will you like that, my pretty Stefano? And what will be Katrina's view on the matter?"

Stefano shivered. The prospect had no charm for him. And how was he to know that Moore was merely bluffing? He had voiced his suspicions easily, and Stefano's manner was confirming them.

"What are you going to do?" the latter asked.

"I am going to wait here till Katrina arrives," Moore replied.

Stefano shivered again. He protested volubly that Katrina, the pride of Florence, the toast of the wine-shops, was not in this drear island. Moore pointed to a hat and jacket of obviously feminine origin and smiled.

"I am going to show you a way out of the difficulty," he said.

"Ah! I am going to be pardoned," Stefano gasped.

"On conditions—on conditions, of course. The wheels of life, my dear Stefano, are best run on the siding of compromise. Before midnight Tosco and Berthe will be arrested red-handed. If you are to depart as you came, I must have certain information both from Katrina and yourself."

"But Signor," Stefano protested, "for so great a man as yourself, so small a matter—"

Stefano finished with a shrug and a smile—a prettily implied compliment.

"There are such things as small matters," Moore replied, "and, as you suggest, I am fishing for salmon rather than for minnows. Now Mefer for an instance is a salmon."

"Mefer is to be implicated in this business?" Stefano suggested.

"Certainly. He is in the business, as I happen to know. Why he's in it, I have yet to discover. He goes to-morrow by the morning express to London, and I shall accompany him. Doubtless we shall have an exceedingly interesting conversation."

Stefano followed all this somewhat lazily.

"But what have I to do, Signor?" he asked. "To give evidence against my friends?"

He paused and shuddered. Not devoid of imagination, those fine eyes in fancy saw a corpse floating on dark waters with a red stain on the breast.

"Not you," said Moore, "but Katrina."

A choking cry burst from Stefano's lips.

"She would never do it," he exclaimed.

"Then you will be arrested and tried with the others. Katrina is one of the cleverest and most unscrupulous women in Europe, but she has a weak spot, Stefano, and that weak spot is her absorbing affection for you. If she fails to do what I ask, she will never see her beloved Stefano again."

The grim playfulness touched Stefano as no outburst of anger could have done. He gave a deep sigh—half relief, half fear—as a light footstep came up the stairs. The door opened and a woman came in.

She had a face of amazing beauty. Strength, resolution, and courage were stamped on her faultless features. But the eyes were melting, and the thin scarlet lines of her mouth had the curve of passion. Her eyes were gleaming now, her lips parted.

"We must fly," she cried. "Tosco and Berthe have been arrested."

"That," Moore observed, "does not in the least surprise me."

Katrina turned swiftly upon the speaker. They were old antagonists, these. And up to now Moore had had none too much the best of the game.

"We last met in France, I believe." The woman smiled. She knew the danger, but there was no trace of fear in her face.

"I am not likely to forget it," Moore said drily. "It will not be long before Stefano joins his friends Tosco and Berthe."

The woman locked her hands together. A grey tinge crept over her face. Moore had touched the right chord.

"You have come to compromise?" Katrina demanded.

"Ah, there is no doubt you are a wonderful woman. Tosco and Berthe and Mefer have been watched ever since they arrived here. For my own purposes I have managed to shield Stefano."

"You want me to betray Mefer into your hands?"

"You have guessed it. For your little tin conspiracy I care nothing. That has failed, as such things are bound to fail, only the law will not be the less severe on that account. All you will have to do is to go into the witness-box to-morrow to give evidence in favor of Tosco and Berthe. I need hardly say that you will be subject to searching cross-examination. You are to answer truthfully certain questions put to you, and those answers will give me the grip over Mefer that I need. I may say that Mefer has not been arrested yet, nor will he be for the present."

"And if I refuse to do this thing?"

Moore drew a whistle from his pocket.

"In that case," he said, "I perform a solo on this little instrument, and a minute later this room is full of police. Before an hour passes you will be in jail, and in the course of time you will find yourselves doing penal servitude for long terms of years. But you are not going to be so silly, you are not going to be the puppet of Mefer any longer. One final word of advice—don't attempt to communicate with him."

It was a long time before Katrina replied. She flashed Moore a glance like sudden death, then her eyes melted into tenderness as they fell upon Stefano screwed up anxiously in his chair.

"I couldn't let him suffer," she said. "And Mefer told me—"

Something seemed to rise up in her throat and choke her. She bent her head forward on the table and two big drops splashed on the greasy board. When she glanced at Moore she was herself again.

"If I were my own mistress!" she said hoarsely. "If I were my own mistress! But what woman ever was who truly loved?"

A stiff inspector with an aggressive Scotch accent was awaiting Moore when he reached the Central Police Station. It was evident that Inspector Lockwood regarded his visitor with no great favor.

"I'm puzzled, sir," he remarked, "fairly puzzled."

"You surprise me," Moore replied drily. "A detective puzzled!"

"Well, it is evident to me that you're not a detective."

"Your information is accurate and not displeasing, which is a quotation, my dear Lockwood. You are naturally annoyed because this affair has been taken out of your hands, and because the powers that be have given you stringent orders to act under my instructions. You have arrested Tosco and Berthe?"

"Yes," Lockwood growled, "and why I was not permitted to arrest that fellow Mefer and his tool Stefano passes my understanding."

Moore smiled with what patience he could command.

"Because Mefer is a big fish," he explained. "At the present moment, Mefer is in possession of plans of the greatest importance. He came here to obtain the key to the submarine defences to Port Glasgow. And, what is more, he's got them. They were stolen by a subordinate official some few weeks ago at Mefer's instigation, and only this week he came over to get the plans. As a matter of fact, Mefer has nothing whatever to do with this dynamite business. He is only using those fools for his own purpose. He would not have the slightest difficulty in clearing himself, and he would slip through my fingers. It is of the utmost importance that those plans should be recovered. You understand that?"

"Yes, but I don't see how you are going to do it?"

"Neither do I propose to tell you," Moore said drily. "I have been days working out the scheme which is complete at last. I shall get those papers as sure as—as sure as you are a detective."

Inspector Lockwood expressed no lively satisfaction.

"It's very irregular," he grumbled, "and so humiliating for me. I know nothing; I can merely produce the prisoners to-morrow and ask for a remand. They have even sent down a barrister from London to prosecute. You seem to have the whole British Government backing you up."

"As a matter of fact," Moore said curtly, "I have."

Moore proceeded to expound his views and wishes as to the future of the puzzling case with a freedom that caused Lockwood some emotion. He was merely a puppet in the game, a fact that Moore pointed out cogently. Whereupon the Secret Service Agent departed for the Caledonian Hotel.

Here a keen, alert-looking man with a clean-shaven face and gold-rimmed glasses awaited him. They shook hands warmly.

"I'm glad the Home Office sent you, McIntyre," Moore remarked. "I suppose you've got the heads of your case from Lockwood?"

"I'm practically in the dark, my dear fellow," the eminent barrister replied. "I know I'm to prosecute two men for an alleged conspiracy, but beyond that Lockwood told me very little. As far as I can see, to-morrow's proceedings will be purely formal."

"I fancy not," Moore said drily. "Do you remember some months ago my telling you the history of that wonderful woman, Katrina?"

McIntyre nodded. A new interest was being added to the case. The interest deepened as Moore proceeded to relate the details of his interview with Katrina and Stefano earlier in the evening. He went still further than that—he told the why and wherefore of Mefer's immunity from arrest, and the scheme he had devised to get the better of him.

"Worthy of Wilkie Collins, by Jove," McIntyre cried. "If Mefer is the superstitious chap you describe him to be, you will torture him almost out of his mind before he and you reach London to-morrow. So you fancy this Katrina will turn Queen's evidence to save that rascal Stefano?"

"I feel perfectly certain of it," Moore replied. "Stefano dare not do so himself, but no great harm will come to Katrina. She can always plead that she has sacrificed the few to save the many conspirators. I have jotted down here a long list of the questions you are to ask her in the witness box. She is a strong, clever woman, and doubtless she will try to evade them. She does not realise yet what it means to stand an examination such as yours will be. Once you get on her nerves you will be able to do anything."

McIntyre nodded thoughtfully. He was lost in admiration of Moore's scheme, its wonderful ingenuity, and the dexterity with which he had worked out every detail in a marvellously complex piece of machinery.

"I never heard anything finer," he exclaimed.

At the same moment a waiter entered with a card, which he placed before Moore. The latter glanced at a pencil scrawl and smiled.

"Show the lady up," he said. "My dear McIntyre, it's Katrina herself. I quite expected her to try and see me again."

Katrina entered. Her face was white and her eyes wild, but she had lost none of the proud, easy bearing. Moore made the necessary introduction, and explained that McIntyre was here on business not indirectly connected with Katrina herself.

"Mr. McIntyre has a perfect knowledge of the situation," Moore said significantly. Katrina bowed. Her quick intelligence had grasped Moore's meaning.

"You know why I come here," she cried. "I will waste no time in idle words. Our conspiracy has failed. The life of one whom I regard before all others in the world is in peril. For none other would I degrade myself as I am going to degrade myself now. For Stefano's sake I am going to be a traitor. I am going to betray those who have trusted me. Ask any question you please, and I will tell you all."

She threw up her arms; a laugh of exceeding bitterness escaped her. The passionate, loving woman was uppermost now, the splendid courage had vanished, a dull shame veiled Katrina's eyes.

"You will repeat your confession in public to-morrow," said McIntyre. Katrina nodded. She had no word for the moment. Her hands were locked together with convulsive force, a scar was on her lips where the white, even teeth had scored it.

"I will say what you wish," she burst out presently. "If I have to be bad, then I will be bad to the core. It is all for the sake of Stefano. Ah, it is only in the South that we know how to love and to sacrifice all to the passion of our lives."

The fit of passion passed, tears stood in the woman's eyes. There was in those eyes the enthusiasm that sometimes culminates in insanity.

"Sit down," said McIntyre, "and let us talk."

Katrina dropped into a chair. She answered glibly all the many and varied questions that the barrister put to her. But out of all those questions there was not one of them taken from the paper that Moore had handed over to his friend and ally.

A fair man with a dreamy face was in a casual way turning over a pile of flaming bookstall literature as Moore entered the great Glasgow station. The man with the dreamy face turned and just for an instant the lines of his mouth grew rigid as Moore touched him on the shoulder.

"Alex Mefer," said Moore, "how are you?"

The man addressed as Mefer smiled. He and Moore were old antagonists, and their respect for each other's powers was mutual. They were both men of indomitable courage and pluck when the pinch came, albeit the famous spy was no less nervous and imaginative than Moore on ordinary occasions. He showed no trace of these qualities at present.

"My dear friend," he cried, "this is a meeting the most delightful. Tell me, have you been in Glasgow long?"

The cool, delicious insolence of the question amused Moore.

"Exactly as long as you have been here." he cried.

"Is it possible that we are both going to London to-day?"

"Such is my intention, friend Mefer. I have at my disposal a compartment in the train, and I have made my arrangements for feeding on the journey. So sure was I that you were going to London to-day that I laid my plans accordingly. Permit me to offer you a seat in my carriage and a share of my luncheon basket. There will be plenty for two I assure you." Mefer's eyes sparkled.

"This interest in my welfare is flattering," he said. "But what do you expect in return for this hospitality?"

"Those Port Glasgow submarine plans you obtained possession of on Wednesday."

Mefer laughed no more for the moment. The sensitive, intellectual face grew grave. Like most really clever men, he never underrated the strength of an enemy, and in Moore he had long recognised a foe of infinite resource and novelty of method.

"So some papers have been stolen?" he asked.

"That is it," Moore replied drily. "I prefer to believe that they have passed into your possession. So sure do I feel of this that 1 have laid all my plans accordingly."

"Oh, oh. You are certain of your man."

"Absolutely certain. And equally assured that before midnight you will voluntarily restore the stolen documents. Come along."

Mefer followed his companion down the long platform, echoing to the tramp of feet and the shrill, smiting scream of escaping vapor. Moore paused at length before a carriage guarded by a stalwart porter.

"Are you coming with me?" he asked.

Mefer nodded gravely. He showed no fear, but he was plainly puzzled. Moore was violating every rule of the game. It was as if two masters of fence had come together, the one with new passes and guards— something absolutely novel in the way of carte and tierce, the other relying on old methods.

"I think I will," said Mefer, "for frankly I don't understand you."

Hitherto this kind of duel had been played in the dark. The right hand of one man was never seen by the left hand of the other until the plot was unskeined and the time to strike had come. Under ordinary circumstances, the last thing Moore would have dreamed of mentioning was the stolen plan.

Mefer flung himself down in the corner of the carriage and attacked a cigarette. There was a banging of doors, a trilling whistle, then the huge station began to slide away. Moore appeared to be studying his paper with great intentness.

"My friend," Mefer said suddenly, "you are not trying to fools-mate me?"

Moore laid his paper on one side.

"I have tried that game successfully before now," he said; "but I pay a higher tribute to your powers than attempting it with you, my dear Mefer. And I did no more than state a fact to you just now."

"But you cannot possibly guarantee that fact!"

"I can and will. I am not bluffing. By the way, there is a paragraph in the paper here that may interest you. It is to the effect that two dynamiters, by name Tosco and Berthe, were arrested red-handed last night, and informing all whom it may concern that the miscreants will be brought before the magistrates to-day. I believe these men are no strangers to you."

"I seem to have heard the names," Mefer admitted drily.

"You came over to England together."

"Again your information is exceedingly accurate. But you cannot connect me with them to my detriment. I am too clever for that, sir."

Mefer positively beamed as he spoke. He began to see daylight. Moore was going to frighten these papers out of him by connecting him with this absurd dynamite business.

"One is loth to lose one's illusions, for they are scarce at forty," Mefer resumed. "And hitherto I have regarded you as such a clever man."

Moore smiled. He saw the point quite clearly.

"I know perfectly well that those people were mere tools of yours," he said. "You came to England with them as a blind to cover your real intentions. I have not the least intention of using this information as a lever to force you to disgorge. You will see later on how that newspaper paragraph forms part of my game. Individually, I may say there are others in the conspiracy who as yet have not been arrested.

Need I say that I am alluding to Stefano and Katrina? The woman is deeply in love with that handsome coward, and she would make any sacrifice to shield him. If Katrina said all she knew she could make Europe warm for you."

The puzzled look crossed Mefer's face again. Once more he seemed anxious and uneasy. He studied the features of his companion intently.

"Katrina would never tell the story of our work," he said. "She would not undo the labor of years like that."

"She may not intend to do so," Moore replied. "But a woman eager to save her lover will commit any folly. By giving evidence against the other two she could shield Stefano. Both Tosco and Berthe are the wild visionaries who are prepared to die for what they call the 'cause.' We will suggest that Katrina turns Queen's evidence. We will suggest that she is examined by a barrister who is fully acquainted with her past, and who—best point of all—knows she is shielding Stefano. Why, man alive, under those circumstances the advocate could make that woman say anything he pleased."

"She will not do it," Mefer cried hoarsely.

"I have already shown you how she could be compelled to speak," Moore said in his most dry manner. "Within a few hours of Katrina's startling revelations every police officer in England would be on the look-out for you. It would be the same on the Continent. By the time we get to London my prophecy will be fulfilled or falsified. If the former, what is to prevent me from giving you into custody on our arrival? If I did that it would not be long before I recovered those stolen plans."

Mefer admitted the point gloomily. Moore appeared to be familiar with every detail of that dynamite business. He cursed his folly now that he had touched the matter at all.

"You cannot possibly connect me with those people," he cried.

"I'm not going to try," Moore replied. "I am merely using those fools as a means to an end. With their assistance, voluntarily or otherwise, I propose to drive you into the tightest corner you were ever in in your life. Then I propose to offer you life and liberty on certain terms."

"Katrina is to be relied upon," said Mefer sullenly. "She will not speak."

Moore looked at his watch. The conversation had been desultory and with thoughtful pauses, and an hour or more had passed.

"When we pass Carlisle," he said, "I will tell you for certain."

"You expect a telegram there?"

"Indeed, I don't. I abhor bustling about when I am travelling, which is the reason why I engaged this compartment. From now till we reach London I don't propose to leave the train. At the same time I propose telling you all that takes place before the Glasgow magistrates to-day."

Mefer laughed, but there was no mirth in it. Moore was getting on his nerves. The train at length passed Carlisle, but Moore said nothing. Another hour passed and no words came from his lips. The train was passing through the heart of the fells by this time. In the brilliant sunshine the green rolling hills seemed strangely peaceful.

Moore watched one of them dreamily for a long time. Then he crossed over to Mefer, and smote him on the thigh.

The whole aspect of the man had changed. His eyes gleamed and danced, his face was pallid with excitement.

"Katrina has turned up," he said. "For the best part of an hour now she has been giving her evidence. The two prisoners appear to be convinced that she is betraying them to save the rest of the gang. A pity that men so brave should be so wrong-headed. Katrina is being examined by McIntyre who, as you know, is great in this kind of case. And Katrina has been speaking of you with the greatest possible freedom."

Mefer gasped. With all his power and strength he was superstitious to a degree. Had Moore some marvellous, occult power of which he knew nothing? Or was he being made the victim of a stupid practical joke?

"I don't believe a word of it," he said sullenly.

"The proof will be to hand when we reach London," Moore replied. "I see you desire further details to convince you. Let me use my eyes for you."

Moore lay back and closed those organs languidly.

"The court is crowded," he said. "At the back of it lurks Stefano, who has been unable to keep away. Pale, frightened, yet defiant, Katrina stands in the witness-box. She wears a black straw hat with scarlet poppies. Her dress is white with red bands across it. McIntyre presses her hard and she shows signs of weakness. She staggers, and asks for a glass of water. She faints, and there is great commotion in court. Then, as it is twelve o'clock, they adjourn for luncheon."

Moore opened his eyes and sat upright. Mefer was pale and ghastly. He tried to laugh, but his thin lips trembled, and no sound came from them.

"Don't!" he grasped with a convulsive shudder. "You get on my nerves. But what you say cannot be true."

"As there is a God above us, all I say is gospel," Moore cried. "By the time we get to London it will be in print in all the evening papers. Meanwhile let us examine the contents of my luncheon basket. In the course of an hour or so I shall have more information for you."

Mefer toyed with the wing of a chicken, whilst Moore ate heartily.

He knew that he had his man now. It was getting on towards three o'clock when he returned to his proper seat and looked dreamily out of the window again. He seemed to be absorbed in the contemplation of a gaunt rock miles away that remained in sight for some time.

"Getting more information?" Mefer muttered.

"Got it," Moore snapped. "The case was adjourned and the prisoners remanded at a quarter past two, when Katrina completed her evidence. She has made a clean breast of everything. She has gone into detail over the murder of that War Office attaché at Vienna. She has given the story chapter and verse. You are wearing the murdered man's watch at the present time, which is hardly discreet of you, my dear Mefer."

Mefer uttered a cry of horror and despair. He clasped his left side, he fell over on his face in a state of absolute collapse.

He fell over in a state of absolute collapse.

A little brandy restored the color to his lips and the light to his eyes.

"How did you do it?" he gasped.

"That secret must remain locked in my breast," Moore replied. "I don't fancy you will refuse to believe in my powers any longer."

Mefer made one last attempt to fight off the horror that wrapped him in a black mist.

"It may all be pure conjecture," he muttered.

"London will prove that," said Moore, "and after London—well, after London the rest lies absolutely with yourself."

The train flashed through the green core of the landscape, leaving the streaming miles behind until the fresh fields ran into lawns and hedges and the trim houses skirting the uneasy heart of London. It was past eight o'clock and the electric arcs were glaring purple when the express pulled up.

"A paper," Mefer said hoarsely. "A paper."

Moore snatched a "special " from the bookstall and hurried his companion into a refreshment room. He opened the flimsy sheet. There was no triumph in his face as he pointed to a double column dotted with plentiful scare heads.

"Read for yourself," he said, "it seems to be all there."

Mefer spread out the paper on a marble table. It was all there with a vengeance. Every trifling touch Moore had foretold was faithfully recorded. There was a description of the sensational witness, the account of her fainting, the story of the Austrian military attaché's murder.

Mefer read it all, crushed in mind and in body. He was the victim of superhuman agency.

"I am beaten," he said drearily. "What do you want?"

"Those papers," Moore rasped out. "Give me those papers and you are free. Once I get those my task is done. And you are to tell me whence you obtained them. If you reject my terms, I give one sign and you are in custody."

Mefer smiled bitterly.

"How can I reject your terms?" he asked.

"I am utterly powerless. My liberty and life are worth more to me than all the rest. Come with me to my hotel and you shall have what you require."

Half-an-hour later and the precious plans were in Moore's possession. They were all correct, not one of them was missing, and there had been no time for anyone to make a tracing of them.

"Where are you going now?" Moore asked.

Mefer was consulting his watch earnestly. He looked half wistfully at his portmanteau; then he shook his head.

"1 dare not risk it," he muttered. "I must just slip out as I am. My idea is to get to Southampton and reach France via Jersey. Good-bye, and curse you for the cleverest man I ever met."

"You have done wonderfully well," the great personage of the War Office remarked, as he fondled the precious papers Moore had just placed in his hands. "Under the circumstances no apology for interrupting my dessert is necessary. Try the port; you look as if a glass would do you good. I am sorry that you allowed Mefer to slip through your fingers."

"I had to, my lord," Moore replied. "Otherwise we should never have got the plans. Besides, he is certain to be captured."

My lord smiled as if the information pleased him.

"There is much in that," he said. "And now perhaps you will tell me how you managed to get your marvellous information en route. I never heard of anything so remarkable in the whole course of my life."

"It was merely a variation of an old fraud," Moore said modestly. "I knew pretty well beforehand what information McIntyre would elicit. As the case proceeded I had it wired to ten confederates in prominent places by the line of railway. The wires were tapped on purpose. Then as the telegrams were deciphered they were flashed to me in the train by heliograph. You see the thing was absurdly simple after all. Had there been no sunshine I should have varied my plan slightly and the signalling would have been done with flags. I nearly frightened my man to death. To his dying day he will firmly believe that I am possessed of occult powers."

And Moore smiled at the recollection. The great personage smiled also, but it was a smile of intense approval.

"It seems easy when you know how it is done," he said. "I am more than pleased, I am delighted. You'll like those cigarettes."

And Moore said it was the most enjoyable smoke he had ever had in his life.

THE ALMEDI CONCESSION

I

"It seems to me, Sir Charles," Newton Moore remarked, "to be a very pretty case. I dare say I can manage it."

Sir Charles Morley smiled. The big Foreign Office magnate had every confidence in the famous Secret Service agent, and fully appreciated his methods.

"It is a remarkable case," he replied. "But perhaps I had better give you the chief points of the matter in question."

It was an interesting story that Sir Charles had to unfold. On the north-west frontier of India lay a large, rugged territory given over to the peaceful Almedi tribe. Time was when the Almedis—born fighters to a man—had caused considerable trouble to the Indian Government. Strategically their position was almost impregnable, but patience and pluck, to say nothing of much precious blood, had accomplished wonders, and to-day the Almedi State formed a buffer against the southern progress of Russia.

The State was peaceful enough now; it was under the suzerainty of England, although the present Prince Kalahami, the head of the Almedis, was to all practical purposes an absolute monarch, doing pretty well as he pleased so long as he remained friendly disposed to the Indian Administration.

In the course of time the ubiquitous English adventurer had thrust his way into the heart of Almedi, and made his home there. He planted tea and it flourished, he prospected for minerals and he found them. The inevitable syndicate followed, and large concessions had been obtained from Prince Kalahami in return for the sum of fifty thousand odd pounds, paid over to the dusky potentate in Bank of England notes.

This little business had taken place over a year ago; then, to the surprise of the syndicate, they learnt that Kalahami had changed his mind and pledged his mines to a Russian company. In vain the syndicate pointed to the fact that they had paid hard cash for their concessions. Kalahami blandly denied the receipt of the money. Certainly a representative of the company had called upon him, but he had made certain fresh demands which Kalahami had with pain to decline; whereupon the agent had taken himself off in dudgeon, and the head of the Almedis knew no more of the matter. On the grave of his maternal grandfather he swore it.

"As a matter of fact," Sir Charles explained, "we are perfectly certain that the agent in question, Captain Stanmore, and his companion, Mr. Rivers, were robbed of this money at the instigation of Kalahami, and basely murdered. Now Russia is pushing in the interests of her company, a matter we cannot possibly permit to come to a head for strategical and other reasons. Unless we can force the truth from Kalahami, things may become serious. If the Prince can be made to confess, Russia is powerless to carry the game further. To find the truth and to bring Kalahami to book is your business."

"My knowledge of India is nil," Moore confessed; "still, I am quite ready to undertake anything I am ordered."

Sir Charles Morley smiled.

"We value your services too highly to expose you to any unnecessary risk," he said.

"Your work will be all done in London."

"I won't pretend not to be glad of that," Moore replied; "but I don't quite see how that is to be done, Sir Charles."

"Prince Kalahami is in London."

"Indeed! Strange that I have seen no mention of it in the papers."

"There are times when the Prince is exceedingly retiring," Sir Charles said drily.

"It was only by the merest accident that we made the discovery. Of course, for a long time we have been morally certain that Captain Stanmore and Mr. Rivers were murdered at Kalahami's instigation. For months we have been waiting for some of these notes to be returned to the bank. One of them was cashed yesterday, actually bearing Kalahami's indorsement on the back."

"Is the man a fool?" Moore cried.

"Far from it, I assure you; but he is a man who drinks immoderately, as his signature on the note shows. That it is really the Prince's signature we have no doubt. The note was traced to a small tobacconist in the Euston Road, who says he obtained it from a dark gentleman with a scar on his forehead who has been a good customer of his. This description tallies with Kalahami, who we know frequently comes to London on orgies of this kind. Kalahami was educated at Eton and Oxford, and by training, at any rate, is practically an Englishman. In those days he was the second son of the ruler of Almedi. There was at Oxford a disgraceful episode in which Kalahami was the chief factor; indeed, he most probably would have been hanged for murder only his elder brother died suddenly at this time, and for diplomatic reasons we had to hush the matter up and bustle Kalahami back home."

Moore nodded gravely. He began to see his way.

"Can I make use of that episode?" he asked.

"My dear Moore, I told it you on purpose," Sir Charles replied. "Kalahami is to all practical purposes a British subject. He is domiciled here for the present, and if you or anybody else cares to look up the facts and lay an information against the Prince, he will be arrested like any malefactor I presume your idea will be to corner your man and blackmail him."

Moore smiled and nodded.

"That is what it comes to," he said. "The Foreign Office does not care to interfere for fear of complications. But a presumably private individual like myself might become disagreeable. On the other hand, I might be disposed to hold my tongue for a price—say that Concession duly signed and witnessed. But that, you will leave to me. Once this is done, we are likely to hear no more of the Russian Company."

A less exalted individual than Sir Charles Morley might have been said to wink. Anyway he smiled approval.

"That is all I ask you to do," he said.

"If I can furnish you with any further information, I shall be glad to do so."

"I want very little," Moore replied, "merely the address of the tobacconist at whose shop the note was cashed and the address of any Oxford undergraduate who was in anyway connected with the mysterious affair at Oxford. Thus armed, I feel sure I shall succeed."

Sir Charles Morley handed certain pencil notes to Moore.

"I guessed you would require these," he said, "and I feel quite certain that your mission will be successful."

II

Moore had lost no time in getting to work. At the end of a week he had all the information he desired at his finger-tips. Three or four days at Oxford had produced surprising results, and all that remained now was to make the acquaintance of the man who was the cause of the mischief.

That Kalahami would sooner or later call on the Euston Road tobacconist, Moore felt certain. For three evenings he hung round the dingy little place, and on the fourth evening he coined his patience into current result.

A short, powerfully-built man came down the road. He lurched slightly, as one might after a liberal allowance of strong waters. As he passed Moore, the latter saw that he was dressed in the height of fashion—frock coat and silk hat—redolent of Bond Street. And the man was an Indian native beyond doubt. He stepped into the tobacconist's and Moore followed.

"A box of cigars, as before," the dark-skinned man demanded. He spoke as one who is accustomed to command and be obeyed. "And change this note."

Moore thrilled as he saw the note indorsed. He saw the sprawling signature he had expected. A little later on and he was following Kalahami down the road. Before the Marylcbone Music Hall Kalahami paused and entered. Moore lost no time in doing the same.

For a time Kalahami sat stolidly regarding the performance and drinking deeply. From his place Moore could study the Almedi's face at leisure. A strong, dogged face—a face hiding vice and cruelty behind a brown mask. The veneer of Western civilisation seemed washed thin by alcohol.

As Kalahami's potations got in their work, he grew noisy. His dark eyes gleamed, he struck savagely at an attendant who sought to check the wild exuberance of his spirits. Two minutes later, a yelling, kicking demon, with coat split all up the back, was being hoisted into the street none too gently. A little knot of people, a jeering gamin or two, and the electric light gleaming on a policeman's helmet, made up the picture.

"Now you just hook it quietly home," the policeman said sententiously, "else you'll have to come along with me."

Moore pressed forward.

"It's all right, officer," he said. "My friend is a trifle excited. I will see that he reaches home in safety."

The little crowd melted away, a pair of regulation police boots clanked along the asphalt. Kalahami regarded his new friend with doubt.

"Who the devil are you?" he demanded.

Moore declared his identity freely. Then he moved on.

"I have no desire to intrude on you," he said. "Out of mere politeness I did my best to get you out of an awkward scrape, and I seem to have succeeded. Good-night."

Kalahami's doubtful mood vanished. He smiled. On the whole Moore preferred the other expression of features; for, sooth to say, the Indian's smile was not so pleasant. There was something diabolically cruel and cunning in it.

"One has to be careful, you know," he muttered.

"I am aware of that," Moore said drily, "That is why I wish you good-night."

The Indian laughed outright. His moods were many and varied. Lack of humor was evidently not one of his failings. He slipped his arm through Moore's with a grip that betokened maudlin affection.

"You're a good chap," he remarked. "One of the best, don't you know. Heavens, if my people out yonder could only see me now! I'm not so bad as you think, dear boy. I've got my wits about me. I'm a Prince."

He drew himself up with a ludicrous gravity. Despite his condition there was a suggestion of blood about him. Moore could easily imagine him in native dress at the head of an army.

"May I ask your name?" Moore insinuated gently.

"Prince Kalahami," was the reply. "But I'm Jones here. Don't you give me away. I'm a funny chap, and that's a fact. Half my time I'm John Jones, of London, and the other half I'm an Indian monarch dressed out like old Solomon in all his glory and sober as a judge. Wouldn't think it, eh?"

"You won't think it in the morning," Moore said guardedly.

"Don't believe me, eh? Come and make a night of it."

Moore declined the tempting offer, and, as an alternative, proposed an adjournment to his own rooms for coffee or soda water, or restoratives of that kind. The amiable facet of Kalahami's nature being most in evidence, he consented.

A little later on he was seated in a basket chair, with a cigarette and coffee. As the narcotic fought down the fumes of the whisky Kalahami developed a certain suspicion of demeanor not unexpected by Moore.

His dark eyes seemed to be searching for something he could not find. "Look here," he exclaimed, "you're not a police spy or anything of that kind?"

"No," Moore replied. "I am merely a Secret Service Agent."

Kalahami jumped to his feet with a cry half rage, half fear. That he had been lured here for some purpose, Moore's manner made perfectly plain.

"Let me out," he demanded. "I will not be detained here."

Moore's only reply was to take a framed photograph from the mantelpiece and place it on a table at Kalahami's elbow. It was the picture of a young man with clear, open eyes, and an exceedingly pleasant expression.

"I fancy you knew my friend, Oliver King," he said.

Kalahami changed from a dusky copper to a dull yellow. His lips against the chrome were ashy, so violent a contrast that Moore shuddered.

"I—I never saw him in my life," the Indian gasped.

"You murdered him," Moore said sternly.

The face of the one-time Oxford undergraduate seemed to smile approval from the table. That the victim was personally unknown to Moore it was no policy of his to disclose. He had the whole story of the crime, chapter and verse, and that was quite sufficient for his purpose.

He looked again at the face of the man he had lured here for his own ends. His features were bedabbled with moisture, his eyes were as the eyes of the cur who is being whipped in the corner, fearsome and yet afraid to bite. And yet there was a light in the vibrating pupils that told Moore of a hatred that could never be lost even in a stream of blood.

Moore lighted another cigarette and resumed his seat.

"I will not disguise the fact that I have been looking for you for some time," he said quietly. "I have been looking for you in the way of business. Your own folly betrayed your presence in England, and my own researches have done the rest. If I choose, I can have you arrested for murder to-night."

The Indian made a gurgling noise in his throat.

"Going to try the blackmailing dodge?" he demanded. "Think I've come over here with a hatful of money, I dare say."

"I think you came over with fifty thousand pounds in Bank of England notes," Moore proceeded in the same calm way. "I suppose it never occurred to you that those notes could be traced. That is the disadvantage of no business training. I could force you to disgorge that money if I liked."

"Take half," Kalahami suggested hoarsely.

"I don't intend to take a penny," Moore replied, "because you are going to pay me in quite another way. Mind you, I have seen Critchett and Denton and Manlove, also the girl Grace Denbey, and I have plenty of evidence to obtain a warrant for your arrest for murder at Oxford. The Government of that day might have chosen to hush that affair up, but if any private individual demands an investigation, no administration on earth could save your neck. Grace Denbey's evidence alone would suffice to hang you."

Kalahami listened with the moisture trickling down his face. There was the same fear in his eyes, the same murder lurking behind it.

"Why do you persecute me?" he demanded. "What can you gain by—"

"I can gain the Concession you gave to the Asian Exploration Company, and which you had removed from the body of Captain Stanmore after he had been murdered at your instigation."

"But I couldn't do it," Kalahami cried.

"I dare not do it. If Russia only knew that there was any chance of such a thing—"

He paused suddenly as if conscious that he was saying too much. He knew perfectly well that Moore was making no idle boast.

"I fancy I know what you were going to say," Moore remarked. "But for Russia, I have no need to trouble you at all. I offer you the choice of two alternatives—the scaffold or the original Concession."

"I don't carry it in my pocket," Kalahami growled.

"I didn't suppose so. The point is, is it in England? If not we can have another one drawn up and signed to-morrow. If, however, the original still exists, I should much prefer that."

The Indian bent his eyes gloomily on the floor.

"I have it in town here," he said, as if the words were dragged from him. "This means ruin to me, but I see you intend to have your way. My address is 17, Clarendon Square. Lunch with me at two to-morrow, and the document is yours."

Moore hesitated for a moment. It was just possible that some treachery was afoot. Then, as he contemplated the ghastly, sweat-bedabbled face, contempt for his own fears filled him

"I will be there," he said gravely.

III

So far Newton Moore had been successful. The case was becoming absolutely prosaic. If Prince Kalahami only handed over the Concession without further trouble the matter was ended.

But would he? Over his cigarette, which he took in lieu of breakfast, Moore thought the matter out. A man of no imagination would have concluded the business with no more feeling than a tax collector. But Moore was not an ordinary man, and his imagination was painfully vivid.

Moreover, he had formed a fairly high estimate of the intellectual capacities of the Indian Prince. The man's eyes were evil, but a light of intelligence shone in them. He was not at all the kind of man to give way without a struggle. Whether he would dare to resort to violence was another matter.

"Anyway, I'll have to go," Moore told himself. "I can't very well back out of it now. Only I wish I had not read so many stories of the diabolical cruelty and cunning of th Oriental mind."

Moore felt restless and miserable as the hour arrived. Had he known what specific danger he had to face, he would have gone to it cheerfully. But he had a horror of unseen perils as he had a horror of death.

His imagination had stood him in good stead many a time, but the price charged was a fancy one in many senses. The price was a heavy one now. With his heart more or less in his mouth, and a fine contempt for himself surging in his breast, Moore drove to Clarendon Square. The locality half a century ago had been held to be a fashionable one: to-day it consisted of gloomy houses, aloof, unneighborly. At the gloomiest and grimiest of these the cab presently pulled up.

"Don't like it," Moore muttered; "it's the kind of place where a man might be done to death and rot for months. How lonely London can be if a man likes to make it so."

He pulled savagely at the bell, and a great brazen discord arose within. A manservant dressed in a quiet livery opened the door. He had the airs and manners of a trained footman, nevertheless his features were decidedly Oriental. He conducted Moore along a gloomy hall to a room at the back which, by contrast, was exceedingly bright and cheerful.

"The Prince will be with you directly, sir," the vanishing footman murmured.

A confidential servant, an Almedi, no doubt. Probably every servant in the house was of similar caste. Moore had no doubt of the fact a minute or two later when the door opened and Kalahami entered.

"I am rejoiced to place my poor hospitality before you," he said gravely.

Moore regarded his host with surprise. The sham European voice had disappeared, gone was the frock coat, gone was the knowing Western manner. In his stead stood a grandee of India, grave, dignified, and magnificently dressed, from his flashing jewelled turban to the pearl-embroidered slippers.

"Your Highness is most kind," Moore murmured.

The Prince smiled, his vanity had been touched.

"Sit down," he said. "There are times when I prefer to play the Prince, and this is one of them. You came here to discuss important State matters, in fact you came—"

"—to enable your Highness to fulfil a promise."

Kalahami bowed with regal grace and urbanity. Moore contemplated him vaguely. It seemed as if this man had changed his nature with his garments. As a matter of fact Prince Kalahami was his natural self. The other side of his life was merely the outbreak of inherent vice rendered ranker by long contamination with what we are pleased to call Western civilisation.

Kalahami lighted a cigarette, and passed the box to Moore.

"I have been thinking this matter over," he said gravely, "and I have come to the conclusion that I had better be perfectly frank with you. You have a certain hold over me which gives you a terrible advantage. So long as I remain in England you are in a position to reduce me to the level of a common criminal. Personally, I am quite sure you have no desire to do this."

The speaker paused, and Moore pulled himself together. Could this grave and stately Prince of blood be the drunken "bounder " of the previous night?

"I have no desire to do anything but my duty," said Moore.

"I quite understand that you have no personal feeling in the matter. Your Government does not desire to be officially cognisant of this matter, so they give you certain information and leave you to do your best. Permit me to congratulate the Foreign Office on their representative."

"Your Highness overwhelms me," murmured Moore.

"Not at all. You have discretion, tact, courage. You have forced my hand and compelled me to proclaim myself as a charlatan, a trickster, and a shedder of innocent blood. In London I am compelled to bow to the inevitable. Out yonder I should have you strangled without the least compunction. I am bound to remain in London a little longer, or you would not have found me here to-day. Do you understand the humiliating position you are placing me in as regards Russia?"

"I am acting from a sense of duty," Moore replied. "I have come here for the promised Concession. Once I obtain that, my work is finished—and my lips sealed."

"After luncheon you shall have the Concession."

Moore was pleased, yet disturbed. This was by no means the kind of man to yield a point in so calm and imperturbable a manner. There must be a raging flood behind those impenetrable floodgates.

Kalahami smote upon a silver gong, and immediately two folding doors were thrown back and an inner room was disclosed. Here an elaborate luncheon was laid out for two. There was no window beyond the inner room, nothing but a small but beautifully arranged conservatory shut off from the luncheon chamber by a pair of ornamental bronze gates. A cry of surprise and admiration broke from Moore. His artistic nature was touched.

"How exceedingly beautiful," he exclaimed. "What exquisite flowers and ferns. Those magnificent gates add greatly to the picture; possibly they have been arranged for safety as well as for artistic effect."

Kalahami smiled as he drew up to the table.

"Safety certainly," he said, "but not quite in the way you mean. The glass of the conservatory is thick enough to defy the predatory classes, but the gates were erected because at one time I kept a pair of jaguars beyond the bars. But the space was too small, and I had to dispose of them. So long as I want to live here quietly as Mr. Jones, of Clarendon Square—a thing I have done on and off for years—I have to be careful. And now let me give you a little of this stewed trout. You need not be afraid."

Moore colored slightly. The idea had flashed across his mind that the Indian Prince might have lured him here with murderous intent.

"I pay you the compliment of taking you for a clever man," the Prince resumed. "I dare say you have contrived to let somebody you can trust know where you are at this present moment. That is so, Mr. Moore?"

"That is quite correct, your Highness."

Kalahami smiled as he attacked his trout with great good humor.

"I felt quite certain of it," he said. "Therefore any design I may have upon you will not be carried out through the medium of the repast. There is champagne, or claret if you prefer it. Prince Kalahami is a total abstainer."

Nothing could have been better appointed or in better taste. The dishes were few, but they had been prepared by a master of his craft. The wines were classic, the fruit blushed, cool and fragrant. The Indian touched little beyond rice and a curry, he ignored the wines; but he consumed four large peaches and two cups of coffee. As the cigarettes came he raised his hand towards the conservatory.

"Let us go and smoke there," he suggested. "You are in no hurry?"

"I can spare an hour," Moore replied.

One of the handsome gates was thrown open, and Moore passed beyond. The atmosphere was hot and heavy, the fragrance of the flowers a trifle overpowering; but Moore had lunched well, and the languid atmosphere suited his mood. The space was small, barely sufficient for two armchairs and the various flowers and ferns, and an old-fashioned stand of drawers on the far side.

"In that third drawer is the Concession," Kalahami explained. "When you leave you shall take it out with your own hands."

Moore's fears had fallen to zero. Nothing could be more fair or open than the way in which he had been treated. He expanded over his cigarette.

"I expected to have had more trouble than this," he said.

The Indian gave him a quick, flashing glance. His eyes lighted with flame.

"I know when I am beaten," he said. "The strong man always does. Otherwise I would have had you removed without the slightest scruple. You dog, I would murder you now if I only dared! As it is—"

Kalahami paused and laughed. The passion passed like summer lightning.

"I beg your pardon," he said. "You will excuse me if I leave you for a moment. Meanwhile you can get your Concession and amuse yourself by reading it, and seeing that everything is en règle."

The Indian crept languidly away. He passed the bronze gates, and carelessly closed them behind him. Then it suddenly flashed upon Moore that he was in a luxurious cage, but a cage all the same.

For the moment Kalahami had disappeared. Moore crossed to the gates in a bound. He pressed against the brass scrolls, but they held fast. He glanced up, only to find that the bronze gates occupied the entire space where a large window had been before the conservatory had been erected. The gates were closed and fast. There was no escape that way.

One moment of deadly faintness came over Moore, and then the man was himself again. He could not nominate the danger yet, but he felt that it was terribly close at hand. It was something horribly subtle and Oriental, no doubt, something that would in no way imperil the safety of Prince Kalahami. The latter was aware of Moore's precaution. That being so, he must be wonderfully certain of his ground.

With white face and teeth set close together Moore crossed the open space to where the pile of drawers stood.

"I'll have the Concession, at any rate," he muttered. "I presume it is part of the refined cruelty of the game to place that in my hands and at the same time deprive me of the power of using it. But something may happen in my favor yet."

Moore pulled savagely at the drawer, so savagely that he wrenched the whole front out of the box, staggering back as he did so.

A paper fluttered to the ground. Moore snatched it up eagerly. He flashed his eyes over the document.

The next moment he recoiled with a cry of horror. He had gone deliberately to his own destruction. On the floor, coming from the box evidently, was a knotted, dull, slimy tangle, fighting and wriggling like great worms. The tangle dissolved into wavy ropes, a score of flat heads were raised and a faint hissing noise arose.

"God in Heaven," Moore yelled. "Cobras."

They were cobras, a good score of them. They raised their hooded heads and eyed Moore with malignant, metallic eyes. A cold sweat burst out on his face, his limbs trembled under him. Many things there were that filled Moore with horror, but nothing to the horror he had of snakes.

He knew what it meant—he knew a horrible death would be his. He could see now how that infernal Indian meant to get out of the difficulty. "Accidentally bitten by a pet cobra," that would be the verdict of the Coroner's jury.

Then Moore went mad for the moment. His sensitive, highly strung nature gave way before the terrible strain. When he came to himself again, he found he had stripped off his collar; the long silk scarf he usually wore was in his hand. He heard a low chuckle from behind the gates.

Kalahami stood there grinning like some hideous joss. All the wild, black blood in his veins was aflame, the man was transformed. He clung to the gates, he danced up and down like a monkey, he screamed aloud.

"Got the paper, got the paper," he yelled. "Are you satisfied now, you Christian dog? Ah, ah, this is something worth living for. If you only knew—fool and pig that you are—if you only knew!"

He might have been whistling to the wind for all Moore heeded. He was dimly conscious that Kalahami was raving at him. And that was all.

As for the rest he was trying, madly and despairingly, to keep the snakes at a distance. It was awful, fiendish work. Those writhing bodies seemed to be pressing all around him.

Hooded heads were raised and curving fangs swooped close to his trembling limbs.

Presently one more agile than the rest rose, darted out a venomous flat head, and struck Moore sharply on the hand.

He screamed and yelled like a madman.

The pain was not great, but instantly the hand began to swell. A dull despair took the place of the madness. Moore knew that his hour had come. The despair turned to blazing anger as Moore met the Indian's mocking eyes.

To his great surprise Kalahami burst into a roar of laughter.

"The snakes are harmless," he said. "They can use their fangs, but the poison glands have been extracted."

Moore laughed gently. Then suddenly his reason seemed to leave him. In a vague way he heard Kalahami's words, but they conveyed no meaning. Moore was seated in the center of a sun-bathed valley, and the tangled coil of cobras were ropes of live flowers in his nerveless fingers.

He knew that he ought to be happy, and yet he was weighed down with a sense of profound melancholy. It seemed to him that he had some stupendous task to perform, a task he was deliberately avoiding. Then a gigantic rose came nodding to the ground, a great, red, perfumed blossom that struck him violently on the head and brought him to his senses once more. He saw Kalahami still gleaming through the bars, and with a violent effort he was himself again.

"What was it you said to me?" he asked vaguely. "Oh, I recollect. You say that the snakes are harmless. You lie, you dog! I shall know how to face my death now. It was my too vivid imagination that robbed me of my manhood. I have beaten you. If I am not at home in an hour you will be arrested. As you suggested yourself a few moments ago, I did not come here without making my preparations."

Kalahami looked at his victim keenly and anxiously.

"You do not feel any further fear?" he asked.

"Not an atom," Moore replied. "Look at me."

His eyes were clear and bright. The man had conquered himself. Kalahami stretched his hand through the bars and touched a cobra. The reptile darted a couple of fangs at his hand. He held it up to show the puncture.

"There," he said, "that is evidence that I did not lie. Loathsome as they are, the snakes are absolutely harmless. I knew that you were an imaginative, nervous man, but I did not give you credit for such a reserve of courage. I have seen men driven hopelessly mad this way before. I hoped to serve you in similar fashion. Had I been successful, you could never have used that Concession. As it is, all the tricks are scored to you. Come out and have some brandy. You need it."

Kalahami threw back the great bronze gates and Moore crept out. He was safe now, but he feared the revulsion of feeling. He clutched at the bars for support and he fought down the rising hysteria as the sodden wretch on the verge of delirium tremens struggles with the demons crowding upon him.

The fit passed away, leaving the strong man trembling. The danger was over. Kalahami's final struggle for the mastery had failed, and he saw that he must acknowledge himself beaten. Better at once to give in with a good grace than face the terrors of the English law for murder.

A little later and Moore was rolling home in a cab. He was still faint and dizzy, but he was filled with a sense of elation and triumph.

"A grand idea for a story," he muttered. "Frighten a man to death or drive him out of his mind with deadly snakes that are really harmless. Prince Kalahami's pretty scheme ought to be used for a story. And I don't fancy there is any need to make a note of the plot. I'm not likely to forget it."

THE OTHER SIDE OF THE CHESS-BOARD

I

Newton Moore nervously fingered the thin slip of glazed pasteboard which was his passport to the presence of no less a person than the Prime Minister himself.

A languid-looking Under-Secretary (unpaid) inquired Moore's business with as much sweet insolence as his manner could convey. The Secret Service Agent handed over the card and waited. It was Lord Westerhouse's private card and bore the pencilled legend "Admit bearer at once". The languid one so far forgot himself as to smile. A moment later Moore found himself in the private room of the Premier.

"Your lordship sent for me," Moore said tentatively.

"Ah, yes." Lord Westerhouse passed his hand over his forehead as if drawing his mind from some engrossing matter. "I sent for you, Mr. Moore. Sir Charles Morley has given me an account of your wonderful successes. I want you to undertake a matter which will tax your resources to the uttermost. I do not apprehend that your mission will be in the least dangerous. What seems to me to be required are tact and ingenuity."

Moore bowed, well pleased with this confidence placed in him.

"Do you know our Asturian ambassador, Lord Walmer, at all?" the Premier asked.

"I have heard of him," Moore replied. "I understand Lord Walmer to be a man of great mental attainment, a scholar and virtuoso, and a brilliant amateur on the violin. Also I have read some few poems of his."

"You have formed a high opinion of him, evidently?"

"So far as a stranger may, yes, my lord. The Walmers have ever been brilliant, and, at the same time, slightly erratic. From what I know I should say there is a strain of insanity in the family."

A grave look came over the Premier's face.

"I fear so," he said. "Lord Walmer has done great work in his time. We still rate his services very highly. And yet lately the conclusion has been forced upon us that Lord Walmer has betrayed—I mean is not acting in what we consider to be the best interests of his country."

Moore's teeth came together with a click. His bump of veneration accepted no impression, even in the presence of a First Lord of the Treasury.

"It seems to me that I am merely wasting your time." he said.

Lord Westerhouse somewhat coldly demanded more light. Moore proceeded to give it with point and vigor. Palpably, Lord Walmer was suspected of betraying the secrets of his country. Such a startling condition of affairs had probably never happened in connection with an Ambassador before. And, unless Lord Westerhouse could see his way to a full disclosure of the facts, Moore saw no object in pursuing the interview.

"You are a bold man," the Premier said acidly.

"That may be, my lord," Moore replied, "but I am not a fool."

Lord Westerhouse drew three skeletons on his blotting-pad, and drew them excessively badly, before he replied.

"You are right and I am wrong." he said frankly. "Briefly, the position is this. For some time we have been doing exceedingly badly in Mid-European diplomacy. This is all the more amazing, because, hitherto, Lord Walmer, upon whom so much depends, has succeeded wonderfully. He displays his usual tact and skill; his dispatches show no falling-off in originality and suggestiveness. And yet, so surely as he writes for our sanction for some brilliant new move, so surely is that move anticipated by the man on the other side of the chess-board. One or two of these schemes could not possibly have been anticipated by a person not cognisant of our deliberations, and therefore the conviction has been forced upon us that the man on the other side of the chess-board has seen the dispatches."

"Have you pointed this out to Lord Walmer?"

"Oh, yes; he is quite as puzzled and distressed as we are. And he declares that the tampering with those papers is impossible. The last dispatch we got was written by Lord Walmer in secrecy; it was put up by himself, it was even posted by himself at some distance from Marenna, the capital of Asturia. Further than this, the letter was sent to a false address, and the handwriting on the envelope carefully disguised. And yet it is absolutely certain that the man on the other side of the chess-board saw the dispatch. Now, how can you account for that?"

"At present I cannot," said Moore, "but it is exceedingly interesting. I presume Lord Walmer told you all this in a private letter?"

"Which letter is at present in my possession."

"If you have no objection I should like to see it."

Lord Westerhouse handed the document over without delay. The subject matter was of no great interest to Moore, seeing that he had already had an epitome of it. He studied the handwriting intently. It was small and neat and somewhat shaky, the caligraphy of a scholar who had reached the age when steadiness of hand was no more. At the end was a postscript obviously written some time after the letter, and added as an afterthought. Moore's eyes dilated as he read the words carefully.

"You notice something there," the Premier exclaimed.

"Certainly I do," Moore replied. "Compare the postscript to the body of the letter. The handwriting is obviously the same, but one is the hand of the present Lord Walmer and the P.S. the hand of Lord Walmer as he might have written twenty years ago. Look how wonderfully steady it is. Even the signature is feeble beside it. I shall have something to start upon."

"You mean that you have made a discovery?"

Moore smiled slightly. His eyes were shining.

"I have made a discovery and a most important one," he said. "I have dropped upon a secret that Lord Walmer has hitherto succeeded in keeping from the eyes of the world. You may see nothing, but to me it is quite plain on the face of the paper. For the present I prefer to keep that secret."

Moore's tone carried conviction. Lord Westerhouse looked at his watch.

"I have every confidence in you," he said. "Walmer has heard of you. and he has asked for your services to be placed at his disposal. You had better go to Marenna in the capacity of an extra private secretary. You will have no difficulty in making yourself known to Lord Walmer, for it seems to me to be unwise to advise him of your coming. When can you go?"

"I can cross over by the night boat," said Moore, "and the day after to-morrow I shall be in Marenna."

Lord Westerhouse looked at his watch again, this time significantly. Moore rose. A hint like that was never lost upon him. The Premier rose at the same time and extended his hand.

"Good luck to you," he said. "And may you speedily get the better of the man on the other side of the chess-board."

Three hours later and Moore was on his way to Dover.

II

The British Embassy in Marenna was a gloomy structure, which might have been a barrack, a prison, or a palace, according to the mood and fancy of the owner. There were large rooms furnished in the style of bygone days, echoing flagged passages, Cordova leather hanging from the sombre walls. And here Lord Walmer lived in bachelor state. No woman would have consented to reside there.

A tall, thin man with eagle features and silver hair rose to greet Moore as he entered. He noted the fine lines of the face, its weary expression, and its tired eyes that were, nevertheless, capable of flashing fire upon occasions. There was a stately urbanity about the Ambassador sufficient to impress Moore.

"I have been expecting you, Mr. Moore." he said. "I presume that Lord Westerhouse told you the exact limits of your mission?"

Moore bowed, and his quick eye took in all the details of the room. It was furnished partly as a library, partly as an office. Books and papers were scattered about, some proof sheets lay on a table; on a chair was a violin case thrown open. And inside was the most valuable Cremona in Europe.

"Lord Westerhouse told me everything," Moore replied.

A shadow passed over the face of the Ambassador.

"I am getting old, Mr. Moore," he said, "and my life's work is nearly completed. Had I not set my heart upon the accomplishment of one thing. I should have retired long ago. And, instead of accomplishing that one thing, I am frittering away what once was, without vanity, a great reputation. Mr. Moore, this maddening mystery is gradually sapping my reason."

"The mystery is going to be solved," said Moore.

"The confidence of youth," the Ambassador murmured, "the confidence of youth. Keep it as long as you can, for there is no more precious possession. I am going to give you a free hand here: you will come in and go out as you please. As to the rest, that is your business. You will dine with me to-night at eight. I have a friend coming who may interest you. I daresay you have heard of Count Gleytrim. He was a great figure here years ago."

Moore had certainly heard the name before. Had not Gleytrim practically built up the Asturian Empire before the present Emperor disgraced him and proceeded to undo one of the most gigantic political constructions of modern times? The man who had once bid fair to dominate Europe had taken his disgrace sadly to heart. He had flashed over Europe a trail of fire with words that scourged as a plague, and an invective like a swarm of locusts. Then he had crept back to the lash of his Imperial master and eaten of the dust of humiliation. A soured man, he dwelt now in Mirenna, forgotten but not despised.

"In fact, the Count lives next to me," Lord Walmer explained. "Formerly these two houses were connected. They were built for the joint heirs of the then powerful family of Valdar. The two young men married sisters and all determined to live harmoniously together, having separate establishments at the same time. How the quarrel arose and whether jealousy was at the bottom of it I cannot tell. But one brother murdered the other after killing his wife. It was a horrible story, and subsequently the door joining the two houses was barred up. When the old British Embassy here was destroyed by fire two years ago Count Gleytrim placed this house at my disposal, and I have been here ever since."

Moore was thoughtfully contemplating the wonderfully carved ceiling.

"Is Count Gleytrim an extinct volcano?" he asked.

"I should say not," Walmer replied. "He is not yet sixty, he is a man of indomitable ambition, and King Otho is dying of consumption. I should not be surprised to see Gleytrim with the reins in his hands again—"

"Then he takes the keenest interest in European diplomacy?"

"He doesn't say so, but I fancy he does. Much as I like Gleytrim—who is a fine performer on the violin—I trust he will keep his fingers off the helm till I have seen that Herzora Boundary business through."

"I am going to ask you to be perfectly frank with me," Moore said earnestly. "Is it not the Herzora affair that you are being so constantly anticipated over?"

Lord Walmer looked slightly puzzled.

"Indeed it is," he replied. "I am forestalled all along the line."

"If Count Gleytrim were in power he would do his best to get the matter shelved altogether? Do I understand that?"

"That is correct. But why?"

Moore evaded the question. He smiled with the air of a man who is well pleased with himself.

"With your permission," he said. "I should like to explore the house. I may be able to light upon something in the way of a clue. I will not intrude upon your lordship again until dinner-time."

The rambling old palace was full of interest for Moore. The legend connected with it appealed strongly to his imagination. Most of the rooms were furnished in the quaint fashion of a bygone day. A film of dust lay over tapestry and carved oak. Here and there were stained-glass windows filling the clanging corridors with a gleam of orange fire or ghastly blue.

But there was something beyond all this of far more interest to Moore. He only allowed himself to simmer in the past for a little time. He came at length to a passage terminating in a large barred door, a door set in a heavy Norman arch, and studded with iron devices of quaint design.

It was the door connecting the two houses. Apparently it had remained unused for centuries, probably since the fateful night of tragedy and chaos. There was no key in the ponderous lock; the iron bands and bars would have defied a siege almost. Moore took a handkerchief from his pocket, and, with a twisted corner of the white silk, poked daintily into the keyhole.

Something brown and oily smeared the white fabric. Then Moore sat down on a broad stone ledge, and laughed gently to himself. Almost mechanically he whipped a thread of tissue paper and a pinch of tobacco into a cigarette.

"Strange," he muttered to himself, "how simple great men are. I suppose they stumble over straws because their heads are always in the clouds. However, there remains a good deal yet to be done. I shall be able to speak more definitely before I go to bed to-night."

In the still, historic silence of the place a sudden strain of sweet wailing music arose. It was a violin being played by a master hand. A tortured soul was struggling there, a soul in pain and doubt, a man groping in the dark for the unattainable. Then as suddenly the chords grew glad and joyous, the house thrilled to a triumphant march.

Moore crept along till he came to the garret library, from whence the mighty music issued. The door was open and he looked in. Lord Walmer was there. As he played his head was tilted back, his eyes fixed with dreamy rhapsody. Beside him on the table lay a rough sheet of notes, and not musical notes either. Moore crept on.

"The man is not on earth," he muttered.

III

Before the hour fixed for a dinner designed to be eventful, Moore had time enough to learn much concerning his host. The diplomatic staff at the Embassy were disposed to be free in discussing the idiosyncrasies of their chief.

There was nothing absolutely wrong, Moore gathered. Only during the last few months Lord Walmer had been decidedly "queer." There were times when the Ambassador transacted business with all his old clearness and foresight. These times were decidedly in the majority.

But there were other periods when Lord Walmer seemed nervous and uncertain. He was shaky and hollow-eyed of mornings; he gave way to fits of depression. Sometimes these fits lasted for hours, or they passed away directly.

A clear-eyed, level-headed young attaché gave Moore this information. Naturally he knew nothing of the source of the evil.

"Any other point for me?" Moore asked.

"No, I fancy I have told you pretty well everything. Most of Lord Walmer's best ideas are thought out after dinner over a solo on the violin. He is a marvellous player, and so is Count Gleytrim."

"A marvellous player indeed," Moore murmured.

"He sits up half the night playing sometimes." the attaché resumed. "When the fiddling is going on not one of us dare go near the chief. His instructions on that head are definite and final. I give you the tip because it seems to me that it may be useful."

Moore had no further questions to ask and went his way. He wandered along the dark stone streets of Marenna. chewing the cud of reflection.

The grey city had thrown off its gloom for once. For three hundred and sixty-two days in the year Marenna was plunged in grey melancholy. It was only in carnival time that she forgot herself and laughed.

The mask had fallen for the nonce. Sober citizens, men of substance and family, had cast aside the black coat of business and donned motley garb. The streets teemed with grotesque figures. A group of handsome girls smothered Moore with confetti as he passed. A clown with a garb like that of Joseph of old belabored him over the head with his bladder.

Moore was in no mood for this masque of flowers and folly at present. Some night when the fun was fast and furious he might be more in tune with the revel. There were two more days of heedless frivolity, culminating in a fancy ball at the Opera House on Thursday night.

Moore turned away from the roar of voices and the clatter of folly, and made his way back to the Embassy. He had little time to spare, for a big, blaring clock somewhere hard by was striking eight when he had finished his toilet. In a small room adjoining the garret library he saw a table laid with candles and flowers and covers for three. Lord Walmer, in an old dress suit and a riband of some order across his breast, was awaiting his guests.

"I prefer to dine quietly here," he explained. "There are state rooms on the ground floor, but their gloomy grandeur depresses one's spirits. You have been out in the city seeking inspiration, I presume?"

"Yes, my lord; and what is more, I have found it."

The Ambassador started wildly. The eager expectation of his face was suppressed as a footman announced Count Gleytrim. Moore gave the new-comer one swift glance, and immediately every detail was focussed on his mental retina.

He saw a tall, slim, brown man, a man lean and hard, the kind of man who never tires, and whose agility, menial and physical, is the agility of the cat. He saw a face thin as a hatchet, set in scanty grey hair. He saw a mouth hidden by a ragged, drooping moustache. He saw a pair of eyes that smouldered. The whole figure was encased in a seedy, untidy evening dress, but Moore could have no need of explanation to tell him he stood in the presence of no ordinary man.

"This is a new assistant of mine—Mr. Moore," said the Ambassador. "Count Gleytrim, will you permit me?"

The Count nodded with a careless, easy insolence, which at any other time would have brought the blood to Moore's cheek. Diplomatic attachés were as tin soldiers to Gleytrim. They were usually pretty, and served a subordinate purpose.

As a matter of fact, Moore desired in remain more or less effaced for the present. He desired to pass as a rather stupid and shy young man, utterly overcome by the honor so unexpectedly thrust upon him.

A couple of footmen placed shades over the candles and set dinner on the table. Moore was alert enough now when he knew that his features were in the shadow. He look in everything, despite the fact that he was more than once carried away by the hard brilliancy and scathing sarcasm of the Count's discourse.

He noticed that the Ambassador was suffering from profound melancholy. His clawlike fingers beat restlessly on the damask, He toyed with his glass of Laffite. but during the whole of dinner the glass was tilted but once.

Clearly Lord Walmer had no weakness in the way of alcohol.

For the most part Moore remained silent. When he did make a remark, it was one of the ordinary flavorless society type. So far as politeness would admit. Gleytrim ignored him. Lord Walmer made an attempt, and an unsuccessful attempt, to draw Moore into the stream of talk.

"I expect you are tired." he said.

"I am keeping my eyes open by sheer force of will," Moore replied. "I have been travelling for the best part of three days."

"If you like to retire," Lord Walmer suggested.

Moore disclaimed any desire to do so. As a matter of fact he had the strongest possible reasons for remaining.

"Coffee and a cigarette always work wonders with me," he said. "If I may be allowed to listen quietly. I do not often get an intellectual treat like this."

A peculiar click of Gleytrim's lips was the response. Moore caught the flash of his hard dry smile. Dinner came to an end at length, and then an adjournment to the garret library was made. Coffee and cigarettes were set out here. Moore dropped into an easy chair and half closed his eyes. but he did not shut them altogether. As a matter of fact he was watching intently. Two violins lay side by side on the table. Lord Walmer took one. and caressed it as a mother might fondle a child.

"There is nothing like music. "he said, "nothing like it to soothe one. What do you say to try that duet of Chopin's, Gleytrim?"

The Count took a second cigarette. It seemed to Moore that the great statesman was regarding him with no particular favor. There was impatience in the glance and something of suspicion also.

"Presently, my good friend, presently, he said in his incisive tones. "I would not disturb the slumbers of our young Talleyrand here. Later on. perhaps, when he feels that he can with propriety depart."

Moore smiled to himself. The Count was anxious for his departure. He had some pressing reason for getting rid of the intruder. As Gleytrim bent over his coffee cup. Moore flashed Lord Walmer one significant glance.

"The violin well played is a passion with me," he said.

Was it fancy or did the Count start and change color? It might have been fancy, certainly; but assuredly the frown and the flash of the eye had nothing to do with Moore's vivid imagination. There was silence for a few minutes. From the street below came the merry din of the Carnival. Walmer commenced to pluck at the strings of his violin. He moved the instrument to his chin and swept the bow over with the firm, straight sweep of a master. A low. wailing melody filled the room, a melody full of tears. Despair spoke and trembled in every chord of the music. There was fixed despair on the face of the player also. He struck a harsh note or two presently, and then dropped the Cremona.

"This will never do," he muttered. "My wrist is stiff, my fingers are cramped. I—I shall do better presently."

Without a word of apology Walmer quitted the room. He was gone for five or more minutes, during which no words were exchanged between Moore and the Count. The former seemed to have passed to the land of dreams.

But he was wonderfully alert and wide-awake. He saw the look of mingled suspicion and relief on the hatchet face of Gleytrim; he saw the marvellous transformation of Walmer's features on his return. His eyes were bright and shining, his whole frame was erect. He seemed to have cast off his shoulders the burden of a score of years. "The duet, Gleytrim," he cried. "Let us play it."

The Count rose unwillingly. But soon the glamor of the music suffused him, and all else was forgotten. Such a concord of sweet sounds filled the room as Moore had never heard before. When the harmony ceased he felt a wild impulse to cheer. He snored ever so faintly instead.

Gleytrim made a half grim pass at Moore with his bow.

"Pig," he said. "It is quite true that you English have no soul. Carry him to his sty and let him sleep."

"No, no," Walmer cried; "he is quite worn out. My friend here is by no means the fool you take him for." Moore suppressed a chuckle. "He is doing no harm there. Shall I play you that Andante I composed the other night?"

"By all means, let us have the Andante," the Count cried.

He composed himself to listen. He watched Lord Walmer with a keen glance and an eager expectancy which had nothing of the musician about it. Moore was puzzled. He was more puzzled still ten minutes later.

For nearly a quarter of an hour the master played on, lost in his music. There had come over his face the rapt, far-away look Moore had noticed earlier in the day. Walmer was no longer on earth. He had passed away from it as completely as if he had won the world beyond the tomb.

He had become more limp and slack as the Andante proceeded. Presently the music ceased altogether. Walmer laid his violin on the table and began to scribble fast on a sheet of paper. As he raised his face for a moment Moore saw that the musician had fallen into a kind of trance. He had seen people walking in their sleep before, and this was what Walmer was doing.

"That's it," he murmured in a hollow tone. "A magnificent idea. If it can only be carried out my life's work is finished. And now to hide it, hide it where even those scoundrels will be baffled."

He stole across the room softly. A small clock stood on the mantel. In the back of this Walmer deposited his paper. He took up his violin again, and as he commenced to play the light of reason gradually came back to his eyes. Gleytrim's eyes were fixed intently upon Moore. The latter gave a strangled snore and rose to his feet.

"I beg a thousand pardons. "he stammered, "I—I have been asleep."

Lord Walmer smiled his forgiveness.

"You are punished by missing my Andante. "he said. "But I see that you do not know what I am alluding to. You must have been sound asleep."

Moore brushed his hand across his eyes.

"I feel quite clear and fresh now," he said.

"If your lordship will favor me with another solo I will not sin again."

IV

The carnival at Marenna was fast culminating in one mad riot. For a time the Marennas seemed to have taken leave of sense and propriety. Moore watched the gay kaleidoscope from the roof of the Embassy, and a longing to take part in it possessed him. At any rate, he had made up his mind to attend the ball at the Opera House. There would be plenty of fun there, plenty of character to study, and Moore knew the value of local color.

Moore descended to the level of the street and stood in the deep shade of the doorway watching the parti-colored stream flashing past. As he lingered there Lord Walmer came in from the direction of the Imperial Palace.

"I must have a word or two with you," he said. "I have been forestalled again. An idea that came to me the night before last has been stolen. And I sat up till three this morning working on another grand scheme—the greatest thing I have ever done. If the scoundrels get hold of that I shall resign."

"But why make notes, my lord?" Moore suggested.

"I am bound to; my memory is not what it was. More than one great idea has come to me at night, only to be absolutely forgotten in the morning. Don't you know how you have strange dreams and strive in vain to recall them afterwards? Moore, if you don't solve this mystery I shall go mad."

Lord Walmer passed into the house without another word. The door of his garret library closed behind him, and Moore saw him no more for the present. He had the whole thing in his fingers now, but one knot in the skein puzzled him. How did Walmer's opponents actually finger the pencilled record of his schemes?

The thing puzzled him all day. It puzzled him at dinner, and it mocked him when midnight chimed out; and at length in despair he donned his dress as Mephistopheles and started for the Opera House. As he passed down the stairs he heard the wail of the fiddle in the library. Lord Walmer would not move from there till morning.

It was nearly one before Moore reached his destination. By this time gaiety was at its fullest. The scene was a brilliant and picturesque one. Moore stood and watched it with the eye of an artist. A little shepherdess, as pretty as one of Watteau's pictures, passed him. As she did so a tall figure dressed as a monk accosted her. The little shepherdess gave a cry of delight; then her eyes grew cold with displeasure.

"Do you call this twelve o'clock?" she asked reproachfully.

"It was no fault of mine," said the monk. "I must have had the misfortune to miss you. I was here punctually."

Moore staggered back breathless with surprise. The sudden flash of inspiration made him giddy. But only for a moment. A few minutes later and he was being carried swiftly to the Embassy.

The place was apparently as still as the grave. As Moore mounted the stairs he heard the wild scream of the fiddle far overhead. For a time he stood still waiting for his courage to return. Presently it came. Moore stepped up to the door, and opened it in defiance of all rigid instructions to the contrary. The fiddler was moving round the room as he played. Sometimes he would discard his instrument for a second to open a drawer, or examine the inside of a spill cup or a vase. The figure of Mephistopheles stole up behind him and touched his shoulder.

"You are merely wasting your time, Count," he said grimly. "The papers you are looking for are hidden in the violin case, which is about the last place where you are likely to look for them."

A snarling oath came from Gleytrim's lips. He staggered back with a genuine dismay as he looked upon the strange, red devil before him. The situation was a real dramatic surprise, for the simple reason that Gleytrim never for one moment associated his diabolical acquaintance with Moore.

The situation was a real dramatic surprise.

"The devil has failed me at last," he said grimly.

"Not quite," Moore replied. "For instance, the devil is going to see you safely off the premises by the way in which you came. I know perfectly well why you are here and whence you came. But you are not going to be successful any more. Long before King Otho dies and you come into your own again, we shall have settled that Boundary business, at least Lord Walmer will. You are not likely to tamper with his schemes any more. Be good enough to take my arm. If you elect for violence you will find me quite ready."

But Gleytrim elected for nothing of the kind. For the first time in his life he was dazed, and just a little frightened. Even an unscrupulous diplomatist may stand in awe of the devil, especially a devil he does not know. And therefore Count Gleytrim went peacefully. Moore led him up to the great door that once joined the two houses.

"You have the key of this in your pocket," he said. "All these big bars and bolts have been carefully sawn through and dusted over afterwards. When you do this kind of thing again, don't oil your locks too liberally. Such things give rise to suspicion. No, I'll lock the door on this side and keep the key. Good-night."

"One question," Gleytrim growled, "Who the devil are you?"

"On earth," was the reply. "my name is Moore. You met me two nights ago. I always sleep with one eye open. And, as Lord Walmer remarked, I am not quite such a fool as you took me to be. Good-night."

Moore clicked the key in the lock and strode back to the library. The cigarette he smoked there was a pleasant one. Half-a-dozen brown stubs lay in the grate, and the clock struck five before Lord Walmer returned. Doubtless he had donned his carnival dress elsewhere, for now he was in ordinary evening attire. He seemed tired and fagged; his eyes were sombre and clouded.

He started as Moore rose to greet him. He regarded the grotesque figure before him with cold surprise.

"This pleasantry is ill-timed," he said. "What does it mean?"

"No pleasantry is intended for a moment, my lord," Moore replied. "This dress has been more or less a part of my programme. I have discovered the thief, I have brought him to book, and he will steal no more of your ideas. Will you be so good as to search in the violin case?"

Walmer did so. His face lighted as he produced some loose memoranda.

"My scheme of last night. "he cried. "I had it a few hours ago, and in the morning I couldn't recollect where to look for the papers."

"Under the corner of the carpet," Moore explained, "I saw them peeping out, and I put them at the bottom of the fiddle case. The thief has been here for some hours to-night, but he never dreamt of looking there. Oh, I assure you I caught him absolutely red-handed."

"And the name of the thief?"

"The miscreant is your friend Count Gleytrim."

Not till Moore had given an object lesson on the door connecting the two houses could Lord Walmer bring himself to the belief expressed by Moore. He listened with deepest interest to the way in which Mephistopheles had brought the crime home to the brilliant and audacious Gleytrim.

"Begin at the beginning, and tell me all," he said.

"I shall have to commence in London, then," said Moore. "There the Premier gave me an outline of what was taking place here. He showed me a letter of yours. In that letter I noticed a wonderful difference between the body and the postscript. I presume the P.S. was not written at the same sitting."

"No," Walmer muttered with averted eyes. "It was not—why?"

"Because it was written cither after—er—dinner, or after a dose of morphia. If I am wrong, pray forgive me, but the latter is my theory."

A pained flush camme over Walmer's face.

"I have been taking morphia for some time. "he said. "You are quite right. Go on."

Moore proceeded to relate how he had watched Gleytrim the fateful night he had pretended to be asleep. He related to Walmer the things he had done and said when under the joint influence of music and morphia.

"Doubtless Gleytrim had discovered your secret," he concluded. "He has found out that some of your finest inspirations come when you are in that trance. He has doubtless often seen you scribble and hide those notes. He dared not touch them at the time, but he could come and, when you were out late, use your fiddle to make people believe you were in and keep them rigidly out of the library till his search was rewarded. Gleytrim knew, for instance, that you would be at the Opera House ball to-night."

"He did; I frequently amuse myself en garçon. I may as well admit that I have a private staircase. Oh, yes, for two or three or more hours a night, Gleytrim could play my violin in this room, and everybody might imagine it was me. Doubtless that is the way I have been deceived. But it was a good job you recognised my voice at the Opera House."

"It was the key of the situation," Moore replied. "I knew at once then whom I had left here amusing himself with the violin. Of course, I guessed from the first that Gleytrim was at the bottom of it, but I did not expect to get the knot undone quite as soon as this."

Walmer smiled thoughtfully for some time. Then he spoke sadly of retiring from the public scene altogether. A man who suffered from delusions was a danger to his country and a nuisance to himself.

"See that Boundary business through first, my lord," Moore said eagerly. "It will be easy now we are rid of the man on the other side of the chess-board."

Newton Moore, the famous Secret Service Agent, came down buoyantly to an early breakfast. The idea of his forthcoming holiday was by no means displeasing. Moreover, he could breakfast for once without his heart in his mouth. In imagination he could see down the Hobby Drive to Clovelly, the lobsters creamy and pungent, the blue flash of old china on the New Inn walls.

Therefore he glanced casually at the roughly scrawled names forwarded to him from Scotland Yard daily. On this sheet figured the names of such cosmopolitan scoundrels as were likely to be of use to Moore in the way of business. The knowledge that this or that foreign ruffian was in London often proved of invaluable assistance to him in his investigations.

Moore made a mental note of one or two names quite mechanically. He had no anticipation of having to use any of them, but this was a habit of his. Then he opened his newspaper and commenced to read. A sort of groan escaped him. He pushed his untasted breakfast away.

"No holiday for me," he muttered. "This isn't altogether a police case, I fear. I may be sent for at any moment."

The paragraph which had so suddenly changed all Moore's views of life was prominently set out in leaded type:

MYSTERIOUS AFFAIR AT THE FOREIGN OFFICE
ALLEGED MURDER OF MR. J. GORDON MAYNE, C.B.

At a late hour last night information reached us to the effect that Mr. Gordon Mayne, one of the Permanent Under-Secretaries at the Foreign Office, had been found brutally murdered in his private room. It appears that the unfortunate gentleman had an important document to dispatch after dinner, and for that purpose retired to the office, which is usually deserted at so late an hour. At ten o'clock Mr. Mayne was discovered by his friend Colonel Constance (who had called to pick him up by appointment), lying quite dead upon the floor and still bleeding from a wound in the region of the heart. Signs of a struggle were manifest, and it is clear that the deceased gentleman did not succumb without a fight for life. The motive for the crime is not clear as yet, for when our representative called upon Colonel Constance, the latter refused all information.

Moore cleared the table and proceeded to study with a lively interest his list of names by favor of Scotland Yard. He had more than an instinct that the matter was going to concern him. Therefore, when his man—an ex-sergeant in the Criminal Investigation Department—gravely announced Colonel Constance he evinced no manner of surprise.

"Show him up, Painter," he said. "You can get rid of that holiday garb of yours—no Clovelly for the present, worse luck."

Painter bowed and retired. He was accustomed to life's little ironies. Colonel Constance came up white and agitated.

"I've come straight here from an interview with the Foreign Secretary with a view to placing this ghastly business in your hands. The Chief thought that it would save time."

"Wise man, the Chief," laughed Moore. "Is the thing in my line?"

"Certainly it is. The reason why Mayne returned to the office last night was because he had to send the draft heads of an Anglo-German agreement to the Premier who is in Scotland. That agreement, though on the face of it commercial, is meant to have an important bearing upon the future of Europe. I need not tell you that Russia or France would pay any money for an advance proof of it. A wire has just come from the Premier saying he has had no letter from Mayne, and the draft cannot be found anywhere. There you have the motive for the murder and the cause. The rest is for you to find out."

Moore looked thoughtful for a moment.

"Of course the police are investigating?" he asked.

"Of course. They may be of use to you. But they don't know anything about this agreement, and they don't know who are the three miscreants?"

"Three! How do you know that?"

Colonel Constance produced a sheet of notepaper. On it in a feeble hand three words had been written—the words: "Three of them." This, Constance explained, had been placed on record by Gordon Mayne.

"That seems all right," Moore said thoughtfully. "It is a good thing you came to me, because I know all the little bands of scoundrels who are on this game, and I could spot the actual murderers in four guesses. Anything else?"

Constance produced the head of a rose from his pocket. It was a red bloom a little more than half blown, and now withered and wilted.

"Where did you get that from?" Moore asked.

"I found it this morning under the table in poor Mayne's room," Constance explained.

"I was trying to find those Minutes when I came upon it. There is just the chance that it may be of use to you."

Moore's eyes flashed.

"It will be of the greatest possible assistance to me," he said. "You cannot overestimate the importance of these brown, scentless petals. Of course I am going on pure theory at present, but so confident do I feel of my ground that were I in Paris, I would go to Charet and accuse him of being accessory before and after the fact to the murder of Gordon Mayne."

"I seem to have some vague recollection of the name," Constance murmured.

"Charet is a picturesque and many-sided scoundrel," Moore explained. "He has a happy knack of getting the chestnuts pulled for him. He knows more of European underground politics than any one alive. At present he is the president of what he calls a Legalist Society with open designs on the thrones of France and England. People laugh at the idea, but at the same time it enables some of the choicest ruffianism in Europe to gather together unmolested. One or two wealthy asses are supplying the money for the present campaign, so that Charet is living in clover over in Paris yonder. I hear his card parties are quite a feature at present."

"What's the rose got to do with all this?"

"Everything, my dear fellow. That is the badge of the order. Gordon Mayne was too austere a man to care for personal adornment, therefore this rose belonged to one of his murderers. As we know, there were three of them. I don't doubt that the other men were wearing red roses also. What I have to find are three men in Charet's employ."

"Who may have crossed the channel already."

"Not they. Every port will be watched for a day or two. For the next week they will lie low in London. I presume those Minutes were in cypher."

"Certainly, but a man like Charet will make light of cyphers."

"He will when he gets the papers," Moore said drily. "I shall have plenty of time to lay my plans so as to intercept them. And now I am going out to have a little chat with one of the murderers."

Constance surveyed Moore through his eye-glass with amazement.

"I never knew you to bluff before," he said faintly.

"Neither do I now," Moore responded. "I am quite au fait with every foreign ruffian in England. This list contains the name of one man I am anxious to see. I am sure he can give me the desired information."

Moore rang his bell, and the stolid Painter appeared. A name, followed by an address, both taken from the Scotland Yard slip, was placed in his hand.

"You know Lebastier?" Moore asked. "Very good. He is to be heard of at that address. Go and find him. When you have done so, run him to earth, send an express messenger with the information where he is to be found on a card in cypher. And please go at once, Painter."

Painter bowed and departed. Nearly two hours passed before a hansom dashed into the street and a smart messenger boy skipped across the pavement. Moore took the card with its apparently meaningless message and translated it.

Lebastier at present in the Café Universal playing dominoes. Seems likely to be settled for some time.

A little later, and Moore strolled into the cafe in question. It was fairly well filled with men, the babel of tongues was polyglot, the sharp clip of the dominoes rattled on the marble tables. Moore had no difficulty in recognising his man playing with another Frenchman. The game was a long one, but it came to an end at length.

The stranger to Moore shook his head, rose, bowed with exaggerated politeness, and departed. Lebastier looked around him for another victim. No other seemed ready to oblige him. He sighed gently, tossed away his cigarette, and gave himself up to meditation.

Moore crossed over and touched him on the shoulder.

"I thought. "he said gently, "I thought it was understood that you were not to come to England any more. Have you forgotten that an English jail is not adapted to delicate constitutions?"

II

Lebastier arose to his feet in a dazed kind of way, then as suddenly collapsed again so that his hat fell to the floor. He was dressed in a frock suit, with hat and boots of the best make. Like most of his class, however, he had no nice discriminations as to the value of a spotless shirt, to say nothing of a clean collar. The frock coat was dirty, and the stalk of a withered flower was in his button-hole.

The small, mean face was white as the dominoes on the table. Moore regarded his victim with grim amusement.

"You seem to be disturbed about something," he said. "perhaps you have had a loss. Yes, on mature consideration, I am sure you have had a loss."

"A loss, M'sieur?" Lebastier stammered. "I do not understand."

"Ah, your trouble has impaired your usually keen instinct," Moore responded. The other writhed under the prick of the gentle irony. "You always were fond of pretty things, Jules, such as flowers and the like. I see the rose is missing from your button-hole. You should be more careful with your gage d'amour, Jules. But fortunately I can supply you with the missing flower; permit me to do so."

Moore took the head of the withered rose from his pocket, and surely enough, it fitted the dry stalk in Lebastier's button-hole. It was a pure slice of luck, but then luck has a way of favoring the man with the keenest intellect.

"You have omitted to thank me," Moore continued. "You are doubtless overcome by your feelings. You lost that rose last night. Dc you know where?"

"I—I couldn't say," Lebastier stammered.

"I can," Moore said grimly. "It was found in the room of a man who had been murdered last night. If I called the police and said to them that here is one of the murderers of Mr. Gordon Mayne, you would stand a good chance of finishing your interesting career at the end of a rope. I may say at once that my appearance here is no accident. I had you followed. And I knew perfectly well that you were in that bureau last night. Where are the other two?"

Lebastier gasped. Surely this man must be the devil. It was useless to try the gentle art of prevarication on one so keen, so discriminating.

"I have not seen L'Esterre and Daronne," Lebastier gurgled, "since—"

"Since you parted with them last night," said Moore, suppressing the delight he felt in the certain knowledge of the other two assassins. "You had better make a clean breast of it. I know all about Charet and the rest of you, to say nothing of your sham Legalist Society. Who has those papers?"

Again Lebastier gurgled. Something like tears rose to the eyes of the scoundrel, his frame shook with an agitation not wholly due to absinthe. Never had fate proved more unkind.

"All three of us," he said in a fixed, husky voice.

Moore smiled. He understood perfectly what Lebastier meant.

"You could not trust one another," he said. "And those papers are exceedingly valuable. You divide them between you, and they are to be handed over to Charet at the first favorable opportunity. Give me your share of the documents."

Lebastier handed over two sheets of paper with the docility of a well-trained spaniel. Moore had no reason to ask if he had any more.

"Where are the other two?" he asked. Lebastier shrugged his shoulders. He protested by all he held most sacred that he had not the slightest idea. He had carried out his part of the programme, and all that had remained—failing this deplorable accident—was to deliver the third of the agreement up to Charet on the first opportunity.

"I fancy you are speaking the truth," Moore replied. "You speak it with difficulty, but then you are so short of practice. You can go now if you choose. I have no further use for you for the present. But you will be watched night and day. If you attempt in any way to communicate with L'Esterre or Daronne you will be arrested. I have spoken."

And Moore strolled away with the air of a victor. Not that he felt like one by any means, for there was much to be done as yet. His mission would fail completely unless he could get without delay on the track of the other two ruffians. If they reached Charet before he could lay hands upon them, then his present success would be absolutely futile.

He knew perfectly well how that class of men mistrusted one another. For all he could say to the contrary, spies might have been watching his interview with Lebastier. Moore's mood was not altogether an enviable one as he returned thoughtfully homewards. The major part of the afternoon was spent in sending and receiving telegrams from a trusted private agent in Paris, who had acted under Moore's instructions on previous occasions. It was necessary that Charet's house should be watched.

One consolation Moore had during the next two days. He was perfectly certain from information received that neither L'Esterre nor Daronne had crossed the Channel. It was a mere matter of money, but no letter had emanated from Charet's house, or been received there without the contents being duly noted by Moore's deputy in Paris.

"$2500 a day is a pretty stiff figure to pay for the privilege of perusing the correspondence of Charet," Moore murmured, "but then I am to spare no money. If I could only invoke the aid of the Parisian police!"

This, however, was impossible. It would be no great matter to have L'Esterre and Daronne arrested at Calais or Dieppe, and searched, but those papers would promptly be deciphered, and in a few hours the contents would be in possession of the French Government. It would be just as well to leave the whole scheme to Charet as that. No, those two ruffians would have to be watched, and tricked out of those Minutes, unless Moore could get on their track in England, when the strong arm of the law could be invoked in safety.

Moore twisted a cigarette, and lit it thoughtfully. For a long time he lay back in his chair watching the blue smoke curling upwards. Directly L'Esterre and his companion reached Paris, they would be identified. The stations were being closely watched. But that would not be of the slightest use to Moore unless he could fall upon the ruffians and rob them forcibly. And again, this would lead to the French Government learning everything.

"I must find some way to trick them in Paris," the smoker muttered.

Another cigarette followed. A score of schemes were thought out and abandoned as being too complicated. The fox had a dozen ways of escape from the hounds, and fell into their jaws at last. The cat had one avenue and escaped by it. Moore's method must be like that of the cat.

The nimble brain was not invoked in vain. The scheme came floating on the wings of imagination. It seemed to Moore that he had heard something like it before, and that not in the pages of fiction. He jumped to his feet with a cry.

"Perfect!" he exclaimed; "and so beautifully simple. Even Charet will never suspect that he is being made the victim of a fraud."

Moore rang the bell and Painter entered.

"We are going to cross over to Paris to-night," Moore explained. "We'll use those clerical disguises— they look so intensely respectable."

III

If all went well now, Moore could see his way to a brilliant and successful coup. He had thought the matter carefully out; unless some accident happened he could not fail.

A few hours later and he strode into a small office high up above the Rue de L'Europe where his Paris agent transacted business. A little man with a mild air and an eye like cold steel regarded him interrogatively.

"What can I do for M'sieur?" he murmured.

"Thought you wouldn't know me, Chabot," Moore responded in his natural voice. "I always find this disguise an exceedingly effective one."

Sadi Chabot muttered polite congratulations. The little man with the cold eye had a vast admiration for Moore and his methods.

"I didn't expect to see you," he said.

"After what you wired me I fully anticipated that you would have managed to capture L'Esterre and Daronne in England."

"So I should under ordinary circumstances," Moore replied. "But I prefer on mature consideration to tackle them on their own ground."

"Still, you can hope for no assistance from the authorities here."

Moore helped himself to a cigarette.

"I am quite aware of that," he said. "The greatest misfortune that could happen to me would be for Daronne and L'Esterre to fall into the hands of the Paris police. I should never see those precious papers again, and Heaven only knows what mischief might happen. Rut once I am in possession of the documents, it will not be long before the murderers of Gordon Mayne are in the hands of the authorities. I only hope the police may not blunder on the scent until I am ready for them."

"You have a scheme, of course?" Chabot asked.

"I have a scheme, and a very good scheme, too. I am not going into details at present, my dear Chabot, but you will see L'Esterre and Daronne yield up those papers to me in the mildest possible manner, and Charet will look on without protest."

Chabot smiled approval. He was a brilliant strategist himself, but he knew Moore to be a better.

"What it is to have imagination," he replied. "May I be permitted to be present when the time comes?"

"I intend you to play a prominent part in the comedy," said Moore. "Can you find me four men who will do as they are told, and who can be absolutely relied upon?"

Chabot flicked the ash of his cigarette. He winked and tapped his pocket.

"You are an excellent paymaster," he said, "and money can do anything. You may make your mind easy on that score."

"Good," Moore exclaimed. "Get your men together without delay. Also, you will have them all measured for a certain garb I intend to have made for them. Then you will arrange for them to be here at eight o'clock every night until such time as they will be required."

Chabot's eyes sparkled for a moment. Here was a mystery, and a mystery was a thing he dearly loved.

"The ground is all cleared," Moore resumed. "In case of accidents, I deemed it best to have Lebastier arrested on some trivial charge so that he can do no mischief for a day or two. Before long, L'Esterre and Daronne will be on their way to Paris. Those two rascals thoroughly distrust one another, and therefore they will probably come over together. If they miss Lebastier, they will be all the more anxious to get rid of those papers without delay. You have made it impossible for my two ruffians to enter Paris without their presence being known here?"

Chabot gave the most definite assurance on this point; as Moore had instructed, no expense had been spared. Every way by which criminals could enter Paris had been closely watched by men who were up to their work and who, moreover, knew L'Esterre and Daronne by sight. Within an hour of their arrival, be it by day or night, Chabot would know. And in this kind of work, Chabot was unsurpassed.

"Well, at any rate, that's off my mind." Moore proceeded. "And now tell me something about Charet. What is the new game?"

"I don't fancy there is any particular game on at present," Chabot replied. "As you know, Charet is playing the gentlemanly Legalist at present. He has taken a magnificent, furnished hotel in the Rue de la Paix, where he holds nightly receptions. Oh, they are what you call swagger, I tell you."

"Half the ruffians in Europe there, I suppose?"

"Not just now—Charet is playing it high, though I daresay it all covers a good deal of rascality. I have no doubt the business you are here on was hatched yonder."

"I'm certain of it," Moore said curtly. "Go on."

"Well, Charet's occupation is at present that of le roi s'amuse. As a matter of fact, he is probably waiting for L'Esterre and Co."

"So am I," Moore muttered. "What goes on at these receptions?"

"Gambling for the most part," Chabot replied. "There are one or two women of dubious antecedents, but the bulk are men. The gambling is heavy. There is a Russian friend of mine who goes there for political purposes, and he tells me it is no rare thing to see thirty or forty thousand francs on the table at the same time."

Moore's eyes sparkled. He had counted on this.

"In that case success is assured," he said.

"Get your men together at once, and don't forget those measurements."

In less than an hour Chabot had carried out his instructions to the letter. Within an

hour of that time Moore had given a pretty order to a Paris military tailor with a deposit on account, and a promise that if the things were delivered to-morrow the bill would not be too closely criticised.

The next day followed without anything transpiring. On the following evening Moore, dining peacefully in his favorite cafe, was invaded by Chabot, the glow in his eyes alone betraying his excitement.

"They have arrived," he whispered. "They came by the Gare du Nord but one hour ago. Then they proceeded after a change to the hotel of Charet. They have been there some minutes."

Moore pushed his plate aside. The hour was at hand, and food interested him no longer.

"Get your men together without delay," he said.

"The men are already waiting at my office."

"Good! Come along then. The comedy is about to be played. Before I sleep to-night I am going to get those papers."

They plunged into the darkness together.

An hour later and five men in long cloaks and slouch hats were creeping along, taking advantage of the gloom. In course of time they arrived at their destination. Moore opened the door of the hotel and walked boldly in.

IV

The arch scoundrel, Charet, was riding at present on one of his periodical waves of prosperity. Like most adventurers, he found life a checkered business. He had known dire want more than once. He had known the inside of a prison also. But he had never reached so high a mark as this before. The hotel was furnished with lavish splendor. The electric lights gleamed everywhere. As yet the spacious saloon was sparsely filled by groups of men who smoked cigarettes and drank iced champagne. Charet moved from group to group, exchanging jests with one and another of his guests.

A large man with a light manner was Charet. He had all the cool nerve of his class, and were he going to keep an appointment with "Monsieur de Paris" in the morning he would have puffed his cigarette and quaffed his wine with the same gusto.

Two or three gorgeous footmen were clearing the long tables and scattering packs of cards over them. Gradually the glittering saloon was filling up. But though Charet seemed to have an eye and a word for every new-comer, he continued to glance with some anxiety at the door.

Suddenly he broke off a gay conversation and started, as his eye fell upon two men who had just entered. Both were clad in immaculate evening dress, and both had red roses in their button-holes.

"At last," Charet murmured, "at last. I was beginning to fear—"

He broke off and edged towards the door. He greeted his new guests with effusion, and kissed them on either cheek.

"The pleasure of the evening is complete," he said. "You have succeeded?"

The taller of the two men nodded. His smaller companion smiled and tapped his breast pocket significantly.

"Everything went as smooth as ice," said Daronne, for so the speaker was. "It was with regret that we were compelled to use violence."

"Ah, I read of it," Charet whispered. "The poor man died. But you got away without leaving any clue behind you?"

"Absolutely," L'Esterre remarked. The sinister smile marred an otherwise not-displeasing countenance. "We divided the agreement into three parts. Has Lebastier come on with his yet?"

"Lebastier is always late," Charet said with a sneer. "He will hide for a week yet. That man was ever a coward. But you have the papers?"

He spoke with the greatest eagerness. He extended a hand that shook slightly.

L'Esterre smiled, but made no motion to respond.

"Later on, my good friend," he said, "later on, when your guests have departed, we will conclude the business and take the money."

L'Esterre lounged over to one of the card-tables followed by Daronne. Charet had no alternative but to submit. By this time the play was fast and furious. A grim silence prevailed, broken only by the shuffling of the cards, the clink of gold, and the rustle of paper money. Even those who were not playing were intent upon the game. A tall man, with a face like a hawk, was winning heavily. An ever-increasing pile of gold stood by his elbow.

"I stake ten thousand francs," he muttered hoarsely.

He won. A murmur ran round the table.

Then the door opened softly, and five men in the uniform of police officers crept in. The door closed softly, the key turned with a snap.

On nerves strained to the highest tension the noise sounded like a pistol-shot. A dozen heads were turned. Charet plunged for the fireplace.

"Police," he cried. "Turn out the lights."

"Stand still, all of you," a voice thundered out. "Stand, or I shoot. Do as you are told, and no great harm will be done. Refuse, and—"

The pause was significant. Evidently the little officer was not jesting. A revolver gleamed in a hand as steady as a rock.

"Clear the tables of all money and cards and seal it up in the bags," the officer said sharply. "Then take the names and addresses of all present."

Charet came forward angrily.

"What is the charge?" he demanded.

"Keeping a common gambling house contrary to the Code," was the reply. "To-morrow you will appear before the Juge d'Instruction in the Rue Maison. Meanwhile, I am going to search you all."

Charet fumed and fretted. This meant a heavy fine, no doubt, but there were urgent reasons why two men in the crowd should not be searched. L'Esterre and Daronne were creeping towards the door. Needless to say, they were being more carefully watched than the rest.

"Those men are seeking to escape," the officer cried, "secure them. They and their host shall be the first to be searched."

"This is an outrage," Charet screamed, livid with impotent fury. "The Chamber shall hear of this. Are you cowards going to stand it?"

An uneasy movement of the crowd followed. There was red-hot blood there reeking and fuming, and desperate courage enough to furnish a forlorn hope, out to defy the law when armed was another matter.

Despite protestations and curses, Charet, with L'Esterre and Daronne, were driven into an ante-room, and the door closed upon them. They were three to three, but one of the police trio stood by revolver in hand.

"Get on with your work," he said. "You are wasting time."

In vain L'Esterre and his companion pleaded and protested. They would have fought for it but for the grim blue shimmer of that revolver barrel. A slight officer in glasses, who had not hitherto spoken, stripped the coat off the back of each. In the breast pocket of either coat he came upon some papers, which he proceeded to examine more or less carelessly.

But at the same time it was all he could do to restrain the yell of exulting joy that rose lo his lips. With hands that trembled he made a show of wrapping up the papers and sealing them officially. The officer in charge of the party gave him a significant glance, and he nodded.

"You can return to the saloon now," the former remarked. "The others have probably turned out all their papers by this time, and thus saved my men in the other room from a tedious business."

It was even as the dapper superintendent had prophesied. A little later on and three officers were placing the whole motley collection in a cab, after which they disappeared with their booty.

"May my guests depart now?" Charet asked ironically.

"They may," was the unruffled reply.

"We have the names and addresses of all of them. They will appear to-morrow as I directed. For the rest I can only regret that I have put you to so great an inconvenience, and wish you good night."

The speaker swaggered away, followed by his slim subordinate in the spectacles. They turned into a dim side street in silence. Then they glanced at one another, and broke into a ripple of laughter.

"Well, what do you think of the comedy, M'sieur Moore?" Chabot asked.

"I think you played your part splendidly," said Moore. "When you come to think of it, my scheme was absurdly simple. We merely personate police officers raiding an alleged gambling den, and those fellows submit with the docility of sheep. Most men are sheep, after all. The gamblers were utterly taken in, and I got all I wanted without the slightest trouble."

Moore tapped his pocket significantly. He puffed at his cigarette with evident enjoyment.

"What about the money and all the miscellaneous papers?" Chabot asked.

"Oh, they were all shot down into Charet"s cellars," Moore explained. "The money will be a big haul for somebody. You may be pretty certain that not one man in a hundred of those fellows will show up before the magistrate to-morrow. L'Esterre and Daronne will be on their way from Paris by this time. Believing that the police have that agreement, they will not dare to stay. Now that my lips are no longer sealed, I can put the police on their track. And a pretty hunt I expect our detectives will have."

Chabot gave a dry little chuckle.

"No, they won't," he said. "It occurred to me how frightened those men would be when they had to part with those papers, and I put on a couple of men in plain clothes to follow them. By the time your detectives are ready we shall know exactly where to look for our men."

"You are a clever man, Chabot," replied Moore.

"Not so clever as you," Chabot said with a pleased red on his cheeks. "Of all the smart things you have ever done, you have never accomplished anything more sweetly simple and ingenious than this."

Everybody will remember the capture of the murderers of Gordon Mayne, and how they subsequently paid the penalty of their crime.

The police were supposed to have done smart work there, but so far as the general public were concerned the story of the red rose and the sham police raid that really led to the dispatch of three infamous criminals is now told for the first time.

FRED M WHITE — A CONCISE BIBLIOGRAPHY

Jim Crowshaw's Mary (1911)
The King Diamond (1927)
Lady Clara (1913)
Lady Edna's Awakening (1920)
The Lady In Blue (1915)
The Law Of The Land (1906)
The Leopard's Spots (1920)
The Lonely Bride (aka The White Bride) (1907)
The Lord Of The Manor (1907)
Love, The Foe (1910)
A Maker of Millions (1909)
The Man Called Gilray (1911)
The Man Who Found Christmas (a novelette) (1915)
The Man Who Knew (1932)
The Man Who Was Two (1921)
The Man With The Vandyk Beard (1925)
The Midnight Guest: A Detective Story (1907)
A Mummer's Throne (1910)
My Lady Bountiful (1905)
The Mystery Of Crocksands (1923)
The Mystery Of The Ravenspurs (aka The Black Valley) (1911)
The Mystery Of Room 75 (1922)
Naboth's Vineyard (1889)
The Nether Millstone (1906)
Netta, The Story Of Sin (1909)
New Century Calendar Clue (1948)
Number Thirteen (1914)
The Old Secretaire: A Christmas Story (novelette) (1887)
On The Night Express (1930)
The Open Door (1907)
Paul Quentin (1908)
Paul, The Sage (1910)
The Phantom Car (1929)
Powers Of Darkness (1912)
The Price Of Silence (1925)
The Psalm Stone (1905)
Queen Of Hearts (1930)
A Queen Of The Stage (1908)
The Riddle Of The Rail (1926)
The Robe Of Lucifer (1896)
A Royal Wrong (1913)
The Salt Of The Earth (1918)
The Scales Of Justice (1908)
Secret Of The River (1934)
The Secret Of The Sands (1911)
A Secret Service (1913)
The Seed Of Empire (1916)
The Sentence Of The Court (1913)

A Shadowed Love (1905)
The Shadow Of The Dead Hand (1926)
The Silver Stream (novelette)
The Slave Of Silence (1906)
A Society Jezebel (1917)
The Sundial (1908)
Tregarthen's Wife: A Cornish Story (1901)
The Turn Of The Tide (1923)
The Weight Of The Crown (1904)
The White Battalions (1900)
The White Bride (aka The Lonely Bride) (1910)
The White Glove (1910)
The Wings Of Victory (1919)
The Yellow Face (1906)

SHORT FICTION SERIES

THE MASTER CRIMINAL (1897-1898)

A series of 12 short stories featuring Felix Gryde, who describes himself as "a really clever soldier of fortune."

The Head Of The Caesars
At Windsor
The Silverpool Cup
The "Morrison Raid" Indemnity
Cleopatra's Robe
The Rosy Cross
The Death Of The President
The Cradlestone Oil Mills
Redburn Castle
"Crysoline Limited"
The Loss Of The "Eastern Empress"
General Marcos

THE LAST OF THE BORGIAS (1898)

A series of stories featuring Professor Victor Colonna, a vigilante physician who murders undesirable people with undetectable poisons.

The Scrip of Death
The Crimson Streak
The Holy Rose
The Saving Of Serena
The Varteg Necklace
The Three Carnations

DRENTON DENN - SPECIAL COMMISSIONER

Drenton Denn is a tough newspaper reporter on the payroll of The New York Post. His hallmarks are a straw hat, a Norfolk jacket, a perennial cigar, and a terrier by the name of "Prince."

The Yellow Moth
The Red Speck
Dust
The Fire Bugs
The Great White Moth

THE ROMANCE OF THE SECRET SERVICE FUND (1900)

This series features Newton Moore, the top agent at The Secret Service Fund.

By Woman's Wit
The Mazaroff Rifle
In The Express
The Almedi Concession
The Other Side Of The Chess Board
Three Of Them

THE DOOM OF LONDON

This sci-fi series of six stories describes a variety of catastrophes which ravage London.

The Four White Days
The Four Days' Night
The Dust Of Death
A Bubble Burst
The Invisible Force
The River Of Death

THE SAGE OF TYBURN (1905-1906)

Each of these stories was preceded by the header The Sage Of Tyburn.

No. 1 - The Chronicle Of The Yellow Girl
No. 2 - The Chronicle Of The Blue-Eyed Syndicate
No. 3 - The Chronicle Of The Inconsequent Princess
No. 4 - The Chronicle Of The Elderly Adonis
No. 5 - The Chronicle Of The Libelled Velasquez

THE DRAGON-FLY (1909)

Six stories about an impecunious but brilliant amateur criminologist, entomologist and ornithologist by the name of Horace Daimler. Each of the stories was preceded by the header The Dragon-Fly.

No. 1 - How Horace Daimler Got His Name
No. 2 - The Three Red Rats
No. 3 - [title unknown]
No. 4 - [title unknown]
No. 5 - A [illegible] Crime
No. 6 - The Mirror Over The Fireplace

REAL DRAMA (1909)

A series of stories published under the subtitle "Being Some Leaves From The Notebook Of A Late Theatrical Agent."

His Second Self
An Extra Turn
"Not In The Bill"
The Plagiarist
The Man In Possession
A Pair Of Handcuffs

THE TELEPHONE STAR (1912)

A series of stories about Keith Marrit, a star journalist working for a fictitious newspaper called The Telephone.

No. 1 - The Case Of El Hamid, The Seer
No. 2 - The Case Of The Genuine Counterfeit
No. 3 - The Case Of The Yellow Car
No. 4 - The Case Of Lord Wintercotte
No. 5 - The Case Of The Rusty Nail
No. 6 - The Case Of The One-Eyed Chauffeur

GIPSY TALES (1903-1916)

A series of stories describing the adventures of a wily British navvy with Romany roots, who is known only as "Gipsy." In his fantasies Gipsy portrays himself as a playwright, and tries to stage-manage the dramatis personae and the situations that feature in the stories.

A Matter Of Kindness

A Liberal Education
A Stranger In Bohemia
Drops Of Water
The Unpremeditated Curtain
Mere Details
Out Of Season

THE DIARY OF A LONELY SOUL (1915)

The Diary Of A Lonely Soul - Story 1 [title unknown]
The Diary Of A Lonely Soul - Story 2 [title unknown]
The Diary Of A Lonely Soul - Story 3 [title unknown]
The Diary Of A Lonely Soul - Story 4 [title unknown]
The Diary Of A Lonely Soul - Story 5 [title unknown]

AN A-Z OF OTHER SHORT FICTION

According To The Statute
The Ace Of Hearts
Adventure (aka A Trick of Fate)
After Reynolds
Alias "James Jones"
An Ally
And This Is Fame
Anonymous
The Apple-Green Plate
Applied Mechanics
The Arms Of Chance
Art Critics
At Short Notice
Aunt Mary
Autumn Manoeuvres
The Azoff Diamonds
A Bad Cold
The Balance Of Nature
The Barrister At Bay
Below Zero
The Better Way
Big Fish
The Big Thing
Billy's Xmas
A Bit Of Egypt
The Black Admiral
The Black Cat

The Black Narcissus
The Black Prince
Blind
Blind Chance
The Blindworm
A Block Of Marble
A Bootless Errand
Brayton's Secret
The Broken Lute
A Broken Sceptre
The Broken Trail
The Buff Gauntlet
Burglar Bill's Pupil
By Grace Of His Majesty
By Wireless
A Call On The Phone
A Captious Critic
The Case For The Prisoner
The Charlatan
A Christmas Bride
A Christmas Deputy
Christmas Cards
The Christmas Carol
A Christmas in Peril
A Christmas Star
The Clock Struck Twelve
The Colonel's Christmas Pudding
Compounding A Felony
The Convict
Coralie And The Pearls
A Corner In Elephants
The Courage Of Despair
Crossed Swords
The Dancing Shadow
The Daughters Of The Moon
A Daughter Of Nature
The Dawnstar
A Deal In Diamonds
Denny
A Derelict In Clover
The Desert Ship
A Dog's Life
The Doll's House
The Dormer Window
A Dose Of Quinine
The Doubting D, or, A Cranky Cryptogram
A Draught Of Life
Early Closing Day

An Eastern Princess
The Eavesdropper
The Ebbing Tide
The Egg Of The Little Auk
The Emsdam Dispatches
The Empty House
An Error Of Judgment
The Evidence For The Prisoner
Excess Profits
An Eye For An Eye
The Eye Of The Camera
The First Stone
The Foil
Forget-Me-Not
For Love's Sake
For Once In A Way
For Value Received
A Foster-Father
Found!
The Fourth Man
Free Labour
A Friendly Call
From Information Received
Full Fathoms Deep
Gabrielle
A Gamble In Love
A Game Of Draughts
A Garden Of Pearls
Gentlemen Of The Jury
The Gates Of Ramshi
The Grey Bat
The Grey Raider
The Guiding Star
The Half-Crown Princess
The Hand Invisible
Hardy's Big Coup
The Heart Of The Anarchist
Heavy Metal
The Heels Of The Dawn
Her Christmas Dawn
His Christmas Gift
His Majesty's Mails
A Hole In The Net
The Hospitallers
Ice In June: A Playwright's Story
Icky Of Oluk Lake
Imperial Preference
In Black And White

In Rosemary Lane
In The Dark
In The Fog
In The Pit
Introducing Mr. Pentsymon
The Joinville Tunnel
Judgment Reserved
Karma
Kindergarten
The Kingmaker's Token
Lady Mary's Bulldog
The Language Of Flowers
The Last Drive
The Law Of The Jungle: A Tale Of Mean Streets
The Leather-Pushin' Private
The Left Hand
The Lesson The Ants Taught
The Livery Of Death
The Lonely Furrow
The Long Arm Of Bronze
Love In Aether
The Luck Of The Game
Made In England
The Man Himself
The Man Who Got Through
The Man Who Rang The Bell
The Man With The Eyeglass
A Masked Battery
The Master's Voice
A Matter Of Habit
'Merica
A Message from the Flood
The Midnight Call
The Missing Blade
The Missing Note
The Mistletoe Bough
Moray The Traitor
More Than Coronets
The Morning Glory
Music Hath Charms
A Musical Treat
The Mystery Of Room Five
Natural Selection
Nerves
The Night Express: The Story Of A Bank Robbery
The Northern Light
Not On The Records
An Object Lesson

The Odds On Zero
One Day With A Working Ant
One Foggy Night
One Of The Old Guard
On Peace Night
The Onus Of The Charge
The Orpheusia
Ostentation
The Other Man's Story
The Pardon
A Parrot Cry
The Path Of Progress
The Pawn And The Rook
Pearls Of Price
Photo By Lesterre
Pictures In The Snow (a Christmas story)
A Place In The Sun
The Platinum Chain
A Popular Novelist
Poste Restante
A Prize Crop
Proof Positive
The Purple Terror
A Queen In Hiding
A Question Of Money
Rachel's Seventh Year
Rawhide Science
The Real Dramatic Touch
A Record Round
Red Petals
Rob Peter—Pay Paul
A Rope Of Snow
Rose Of The Desert
A Royal Bag
The Royal Train
The Salmon Poachers
Santa Anna
A Satisfactory Reference
Saviour From The North
The Second Chapter
Second In The Field
The Shebeeners
A Single Hair
Sir Jeremiah's Big Shoot
Sister Louise
The Sixteenth Chapter
A Sleeping Partner
Sleeping Partner

A Sound In The Night
"Special" To The Telephone
A Stolen Interview
The Straight Game
The Stranger Within The Gate
Sub Rosa
The Substitute
The Superman
The Supreme Test
The Sword Of Justice
A Table Tragedy
The Thirty-Seventh Month
This Little World
A Thrilling Exit
The Throat Of The Wolf
The Ticket
To Be Let Furnished
Treasures Three
The Two Bon-Bons
Two Of Them
The Unbelieving Eye
Unbidden Guests
The Unexpected
An Unrecorded Crime
The Vital Spark
The Vital Spot
War Ribbons
The Waterwitch
The Western Way
When The Moon Set
The White Geranium
The White Spot
White Wings (1922)
The Wings Of Chance (1922)
The Witness (1920)
The World Next Door (1916)